DEMON

STATE

DEMON
STATE

a Fable by

JAKE PAGE

W · W · NORTON & COMPANY
NEW YORK · LONDON

FIRST EDITION

The text of this book is composed in Baskerville, with display type set in
Ivy League. Composition and manufacturing by the Maple Vail Book
Manufacturing Group.

BOOK DESIGN BY MARJORIE J. FLOCK

Library of Congress Cataloging in Publication Data
Page, Jake.
  Demon state.
  I. Title.
PS3566.A333D4   1985   813'.54   85-11431

ISBN 0-393-02245-5

W. W. Norton & Company, Inc., 500 Fifth Avenue, New York, N.Y. 10110
W. W. Norton & Company Ltd., 37 Great Russell Street, London WC1B 3NU

1 2 3 4 5 6 7 8 9 0

C 7695

for Susanne

DEMON

STATE

1 MORE THAN LIKELY, you won't believe this. I'm not sure *I* believe it even though I went through the whole damn thing from its beginning in an Irish pub in Portland to the time we went to Seattle in the spring and I went hunting.

What's hard to believe is not that she did what she did for all of us. I understand what she was doing and how it worked. I saw the results before I really understood the technique. For example, she turned a gentle giant, Mo Flynn, into a terror. The guy had been scared that his shadow might hurt someone and he had never been particularly effective, but when she got through with him he was a terrorist for an average of thirty-eight minutes a night. The same for all of us—or most of us anyway. I understand what she was doing. What I still don't understand is why she started in the first place, but who cares now that it is all settled.

Her name is Kendall Lea. She grew up in a Westchester suburb of New York and went to college in Massachusetts at some one of those Ivy League women's colleges, Mount Holyoke, I think. She told me in Scottsdale one night in a restaurant called The Famous Pacific Seafood Company, best damn oysters I've ever eaten even though there aren't any natural-born oysters within a thousand miles, and I was so excited by the oysters that I forgot to concentrate on the name of the college. I think it was Mount Holyoke but I could be wrong.

When she told me, in the fish place, I'd gotten to know her a little and didn't hang on every word she said the way you do when you first meet someone and fall in love like falling down a well. You don't know there's a well there in front of you and all of a sudden you step into it and—bang!—you're in love.

Anyway, Kendall Lea is about five-foot-eight with blond hair. She usually wears it down around her shoulders, straight, the true stuff, none of those ugly curling irons. She has a quiet face—that's the best way to say it and I've thought about that a lot—always at peace, even if she was raising her eyebrows or laughing at the guys with that lightly lipsticked, wide mouth. Her eyes are the thing that gets you.

Sapphires.

If you've ever really looked at dark blue sapphires, you'll know what I mean.

Five-foot-eight on a woman is big but around us she didn't look big. Just sufficient. Strong. You knew perfectly well she could change a tire on a truck as easily as she could hand you a glass of wine.

She has a hell of a figure—not your typical pin-up figure but ample. Lithe. Thin legs and a lot of shoulder and boobs. Makes you think of a racehorse—a thoroughbred—and of course that's what she is, what with her upbringing. Her dad's a banker in New York and her mother, as I remember it, ran the county's United Appeal for a thousand years. Aristocratic. That's why I wonder why she wanted to mess around with us—a bunch of college-educated dummies, media-meat, robots in the service of American professional athletics and commerce: the Albuquerque Demons.

When I met Kendall Lea in the Irish pub in Portland—
Moriarity's it's called and it has a lot of dark wood paneling
and brass and green decorations and a halfway decent Irish
band in which one guy plays a tambourine-shaped drum
with what looks like a wooden salad spoon and it drives me
wild—anyway, when I met Kendall Lea there, the Albuquerque Demons had just lost their fifth game in a row,
112–87, and we were in last place.

The coach, Big Jim Munson, a red-haired slab of con-
crete with no sense of humor and an awkward way of dealing with people but one of the great strategists of the game—
but what can a strategist do with troops like the Demons?—
Big Jim simply walked out of the arena. Never stopped at
the locker room. I guess there was nothing he could say.
He just went to his hotel room.

The guys had put on a little spurt at the end and had
narrowed Portland's lead to eleven points. Then they gave
up and Portland outscored them 16–2 in the last five minutes and Big Jim just left without a word. Three wins and
sixteen losses. Last in the league. It's the kind of start that
makes a man shit rabbit pellets and both Big Jim's contract
and mine—I'm assistant coach—were up at the end of the
season, not that owners can't sack you anytime they choose.

At the time, the owner of the Albuquerque Demons, a
man named Charles (Tub) Bligh, as they put it in the newspapers, was in Germany, making a deal to sell molybdenum which he mines in the Rockies west of Denver and
had too much of, the steel industry having gone to hell and
molybdenum being some kind of alloy that makes steel hard.
Anyway I was glad that Tub Bligh was thousands of miles
away and probably wouldn't know until the next day that
his team and his coaching staff had once again let him down,
embarrassed him before his peers, made him the laughing-

stock of his men's club and all that.

Usually, after a loss on the road, the phone rings in the locker room and Big Jim answers it, knowing it's Tub Bligh, sitting in his big, mahogany-paneled study and watching the 60-inch TV screen, and Big Jim always knows what Tub will say. "Well, the guys looked good there for a few minutes, Jim," Tub will say, "but they sure fell apart. What are we going to do about that?"

And Big Jim, his face pale with defeat but reddening with the seething kind of anger that only a coach can experience, or maybe a parent who's done his best to raise the kids he got and turned them loose in the world and watches them screw up—Big Jim doesn't say what he really means, which is that if Tub would open up his wallet a little wider and buy up some of the league's talent, the Demons could get respectable. Instead Big Jim talks about injuries that are holding us back and how the next day we'll get back at work getting the guys habituated to the basics, to the simple strategies that could win ball games if well executed, if the guys only concentrated.

That night in Portland, Big Jim probably figured there would be no phone call, Tub being in Germany, and went home. I did go to the locker room and tried to cheer the guys up—they had walked off the court with the kind of slump to their shoulders that looked dangerous to me—defeated not just in Portland but in spirit—and I thought it would be a good idea to say a few technical things to them about tightening up this and loosening up that and how they were getting there, just a few more weeks of concentration and all that cheerleading stuff, and the phone rang.

It was Tub Bligh.

"Hello, Mr. Bligh," I said.

"Well the guys looked pretty good out there for a few

minutes," said Tub Bligh. "But they sure as hell fell apart at the end. What are we going to do about that?"

"Well, Mr. Bligh, we're working on basics and it's going to take a little time."

"Basics. Yeah. Well, keep working on the basics." His voice sounded like a distant swarm of bees. "I'll be back in a couple of days."

I hung up the phone, turned to the sweaty men, great gangling geeks who were slumped in front of the foreign lockers, and said: "Okay, the plane leaves at ten tomorrow morning. We've got a practice in Seattle at four. There's a couple of things I want to show you."

And I left the locker room with the sense that no matter what I did, the season was already over. The rest would be playacting.

Four years earlier, the Demons had won it all. Best record in the West, on to the play-offs where we had iced San Antonio, beat Los Angeles in seven games, and took the Knicks in five. Champions. All of Albuquerque went ape for two weeks.

Of course, I wasn't with the team then and neither was Big Jim Munson. After the championship season the team fell apart. It had revolved around three key players. One of these, Jeris Williams, retired after he got his championship ring. He had been the shortest (six-eight) and most horrendously physical center in the league, and a thirty-five-year-old sledgehammer. Jeris was a master at setting picks, where you stand in a place you know some opposing player needs to go, and either they run into you or they get the hell out of the way. With Jeris, who could establish ownership of a spot on the floor so quickly you didn't know he was standing still, people learned to keep well away so they wouldn't lose their teeth or other valuable equipment.

It was like running into the side of a truck.

No one ever asked what Jeris Williams did under the basket and the referees never could figure it out, but a lot of guys—especially in that championship season—limped off the floor. One of the keys to winning basketball games is getting rebounds, particularly offensive rebounds. Most teams make about 50 percent of their shots on the average. If, on the 50 percent that you miss, you get the rebound, then you've got nother fifty-fifty chance of scoring two points. Jeris Williams led the league in offensive rebounds for seven of his thirteen years in the league.

He played his last season in agony. The X rays of his knees looked like a Jell-o commercial and the pain was finally more than even Jeris could take. Hardwood floors are particularly mean to the big guys. So he retired. He lives outside Albuquerque and runs a school for little kids, and comes to most of the home games.

While Jeris Williams was scaring the hell out of everyone on the basketball court that year, they were baffled by Phil Clew. Phil was the point guard, the playmaker who brings the ball down court and gets things going. No one on the opposing team ever knew what Phil had in mind at any given moment. I've never seen anyone else who could have 95 percent of his body going left and wind up going right, charging toward the other team's biggest guy, leap, hang in the air like a cloud and, still airborne, dip under the hoop and flip the ball up and in over his shoulder. It was aerodynamically impossible, the way engineers tell you that bumblebees can't fly, and it was sheer ballet. And when the traffic was heavy, Phil had an uncanny ability to pass the ball to the one man on his team who at the moment was about to break free. He led the league in assists that season. And then, that summer after the season was over, he got hit by a drunk in a car and is a paraplegic, aged twenty-seven.

With these two guys out of the line-up, it was clearly what we in sports call rebuilding time. And it was also a time of growing recession so Tub Bligh, even though he was riding high on the championship, kept talking about the slow demand for molybdenum so he couldn't afford to buy big talent. And because the Demons had won it all, they got to pick last in the drafting of college players and wound up with mediocre new guys from that. So they became a losing team, finishing eighth in the West and out of the play-offs.

The other standout on the championship team was Raphael Flint, a six-ten power forward who was second only to Jeris Williams in rebounding, and who led the league in all-time minutes played as well as being one of its top scorers. Raphael, aged thirty-two, which is getting on for a basketball player, let it be known through the newspapers that he wanted to be traded once the team fell apart. Well, Tub Bligh wasn't about to trade away the only drawing card he had on the team. Furthermore, Raphael had two more years to go on a very expensive contract and not many teams want to pay that much for an aging superstar. So Tub just traded everyone else and wound up with a couple of promising kids in the draft.

And he hired Big Jim Munson away from Utah to be the Demon coach. And Big Jim called me up in my apartment in Denver and said I was his assistant coach. Munson had played for Chicago long ago and he was a fierce man who had never forgotten a thing about basketball. He'd blown out of the NBA when he leapt with some vengeance after a larger, more skillful center and wound up with a skull fracture, having thrown his 240 pounds into the steel stanchion that keeps the glass backboard up there. He had been my coach at the University of Colorado and had turned a third-rate college team into a near winner.

I was six-five at the time (I later grew to six-six) and had played both small forward and shooting guard for Big Jim. I wasn't really all that good athletically but in that league I was good enough and I could make up for lack of skill with what I was told is an intuitive understanding of the game and the patterns as they change every second during the game. I knew the moves and even if I was a little late making them, they still worked.

I also learned the dirty parts, fooling the refs, playing psychological games on the rubes underneath the basket until they got so mad they did something dumb enough for the refs to see. After college, I got drafted by the New Jersey Nets, not for very much even in those days, and married a University of Colorado girl named Ellie and went off to play pro ball.

After three years of that—I wasn't really fast enough to be a shooting guard or big enough to play forward—and after being traded twice, to Utah and then San Diego, I quit and went into business. Real estate. I'd taken a business degree at Colorado and I tried it out. Ellie was happy but I wasn't. She thought basketball was dumb, a bunch of sweaty thugs playing a boy's game, and I thought real estate was terminally boring. We fought a lot while I worked for the real estate firm and when Big Jim Munson called and said I was his assistant coach, I said, without thought, "Okay, Coach. I'll be down there tomorrow."

It was after the Demons' second road trip that season, during which we lost six games in a row, that I returned to find a note from Ellie saying, "I know that basketball means more to you than I do. Maybe I smell wrong. Have a great time, but I quit."

Actually Ellie smelled wonderful, but I haven't seen her since and that was two years ago. She didn't take anything much out of the apartment. We really didn't have very much in it. She went to southern California and probably roots for the damn Lakers. As I say, I haven't heard from her.

I didn't even fool around on those first two road trips.

Loyal, faithful, and true—that's me. Like a Boy Scout. I had been a Boy Scout, in fact, went from my Eagle badge to my Bear badge faster than any kid in Colorado that year. I was faithful to Ellie but I guess I gave her a lot of trouble. I don't really like to talk about Ellie or those few years because I feel dumb about it. You've got to do what you've got to do, but I look on my need to pursue basketball a little differently than I look on a sudden (probably predictable) big loud NO that I received from Ellie. People who say no that loud soon leave my mind, especially when I feel a little guilty in the bargain.

Probably if I'd become a forest ranger and lived in some goddamned little cabin, Ellie would have been happy raising babies and stoking the woodstove and would have thought I was a proper hero for saving the trees and all that. When I was growing up in Rifle, up in northwestern Colorado, I did think about being a forest ranger, but then I got basketball on my mind. I like the game. I like the movement, the strategies, the smells even (dirty socks was what Ellie was referring to in her curt little letter, the smell of the locker room).

Anyway, in the off-season I still go out with a pack and wander in the Rockies where it's quiet and, to me, beautiful. I know guys who hate mountains, hate woods, hate all that stuff. They grew up in cities and most of the ones I know like that are basketball players. They're missing something. So is anyone who spends all the time in cities.

So here I am—living in cities and I mean lots of cities for most of the year, and the one I hate the most is Los Angeles because I'm sure that Ellie is sitting somewhere in the seats even though she hates basketball, so she can laugh about how triumphantly I returned to the game I love and wound up with a bunch of losers.

2 PEOPLE in basketball like to talk about it a lot, as you may have noticed, and you'll have to forgive me if I go on a little longer before I tell you about Kendall Lea because you can't really know what she did without knowing about us.

Fundamentals are everything in basketball and the most fundamental thing about basketball is that you've got five guys on the floor at any moment. Generally, you want them all running around in some kind of bewildering mixup but they start from a basic configuration of two forwards, one center, and two guards. Diagramatically it looks like this:

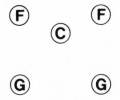

The forwards are usually big, the center bigger, and the guards smaller.

Anyone who has turned the channel-changer from *The Fall Guy* to the movie has probably interrupted a basketball game and seen a coach during a time-out with a clipboard frantically diagramming plays from this basic arrangement of forwards, guards, and center. There are other clowns around the court in stripes called referees, but it is from this basic configuration that strategists like Big Jim and General Patton do their thing. Here are the people we had to fill in the blanks on the diagram that year when we found ourselves in Portland and in last place.

We had Raphael Flint, whom I've mentioned already. He plays power forward. He's six-ten and big. At power forward you need a man who can push people around under the basket, let them know they're going to pay in accumulated pain for whatever they do, a guy who has at least two unstoppable moves, like *owning* the basket if he's ten feet out with his back turned to it. He's got to get rebounds at both ends of the floor. You need an alpha male who will let no challenge go unmet. Good power forwards have a way of symbolically peeing on their territories around the hoop and their lesser opponents have a way of giving up in some deep-seated manner before the first whistle blows. Raphael Flint knew all of that from his first game in the NBA twelve years before and he had glared at his opponents in such a way that they knew just where Raphael's territory was and how much it would hurt if they seriously challenged his possession of it.

Raphael had a beautiful, soft turn-around jump shot, a joy to behold. He could do the other stuff, slam dunking and all, and he used them but he really preferred simply to stick out his ass, jig around, turn and humiliate the defender with that simple jumper.

But when you're thirty-two years old and coaches have found you're a little slower than three years ago and know that a sagging defense can now upset the old rhythm, then the turn-around jumper gets a bit less effective. And if you are of a mind to insist that you are there primarily for that shot, the guards don't get you the ball as often and you get grumpy. Raphael Flint had been found out by the league's coaches. He'd lost a half a step and while he was still one of the strongest forwards in the league, they had figured him out—first the opponents, then his own teammates, and he didn't get the ball as much anymore. In this season I'm talking about Raphael was in a monumental grump. His defense was still devastating but on offense he was less productive than in any previous season. He wanted to be traded, especially to Phoenix, where he'd played in college, but Tub still wanted him and Phoenix didn't.

You couldn't talk to Raphael about any of this. He would simply recite the team's record and say: "If those dipshit guards would get me the ball, we'd be okay." Glare. And so, for the first part of the season, he haunted his chosen quadrant of the court, waited for the ball to come his way, and occasionally in a supreme grouch would foul out, hammering some youth and stalking off the court with nothing but a glance at the clock, as if to say that now he was out of the game it was all over.

"What the hell are we going to do about Raphael?" Big Jim had asked me earlier that season in Washington's National Airport one morning where we were waiting for the plane to Boston. A couple of the guys were pawing over stuff in a little store nearby and people were gawking at them. Ninety senators could walk through National Airport all at once and no one would notice, but run a basketball team through and everyone stares. Of course they do. Everyone stares at freaks.

"You can't bench him, Coach."

"I can bench anyone," said Big Jim, his large flat fingers curled around a white coffee mug.

"He won't do anything, coming off the bench," I said.

"Yeah. You're right. And Mo Flynn would piss green if he had to start." Big Jim stared at the dark, greasy surface of his coffee. "Mo Flynn pisses green anyway."

"Is he not Irish?" I asked in a brogue.

"This is serious. We're losing left and right." Big Jim's brow became a set of flaming red furrows.

It was Mo Flynn that was most on our minds in those days, our sixth man, the guy we sent in to relieve either Raphael or Del Babbitt, the center. Babbitt was seven feet tall but he wasn't as strong as most of the NBA centers. He had a nice soft outside shot and a few good moves but he was generally overpowered by opposing centers and now, after two years in the league, he kind of knew he was over-powered and so he played a loose game, out from the hoop, and as a result we were missing rebounds at both ends, especially when Raphael was in a snit.

You'd think, maybe, that the coaching staff could simply tell these monsters what to do and they would do it, but the game is not like that. Five guys on the team each made more money than the whole coaching staff put together. They all had contracts that said that Tub Bligh was going to pay their salaries whether they played or not and so these guys each became domains unto themselves. The coaches can persuade, suggest, but they cannot demand or auto-matically get obedience. Most of the job of being a coach is to inspire and teach, mostly inspire, and that year Big Jim and I were about as good at inspiring as a dachshund is at pulling a farm wagon.

We knew the weaknesses of each guy on the team before we—or they—got there, and every player has some weak-ness, no matter how good he is, but the major disappoint-ment was Mo Flynn. His weaknesses had surprised us. Mo Flynn was meat. I mean Meat. He was six-eleven, weighed two thirty, could run in short bursts faster than anyone his size I've ever seen, and could jump so his shoes were four feet off the floor. You'd look at Mo Flynn and you wouldn't see the muscle—he was covered by a permanent layer of baby fat or something. He looked soft till you ran into him.

Flynn was smart, too, he could see the whole court at once and knew how to get the ball on its way to the open men before the man was obviously going to be open. But Mo had a tragic flaw, at least tragic for a basketball player. He didn't like to use his strength. He would back off a little. He was, we learned later, terrified of his strength and had worried in the back of his mind ever since he was a kid, an overgrown kid, that he would hurt someone by mistake. It happens to some big guys.

Mo was never intimidated on the court by his opponents, he was intimidated by himself and so he didn't do much for us.

Mo Flynn had come out of the Ivy League, a place that doesn't provide the world with much in the way of players (except Bill Bradley and a few others like that—cerebral players) but he had dominated that league while he was at Princeton, and maybe no one thought during the draft that a guy who's that big and good can dominate such a league without using his strength. Anyway, we drafted Flynn the year before to back up Raphael and eventually take his place and it was frustrating as hell to see all that good meat going to waste. He was adequate. That's all. Raphael thought he was ridiculous. Raphael was a street-toughened thug from Detroit who knew that muscle was created for warfare, and behind Mo's back referred to him as the "egghead fag" and a few other epithets mostly related to poultry and defecation.

Running a basketball team is like operating a full-time kindergarten.

Then there was Fast Fred Spokes, six-seven and the finest offensive forward to ever come out of Bowling Green, slick, fast, quick to jump, and gentle as he flew through the air. Only problem was he couldn't play defense and if the opposing forward was an inch or two bigger or a degree more desirous, Fast Fred missed the hoop and the rebound.

Fast Fred was a showboat who had impressed Tub but he was not the exact thing you wanted in a small forward, which is someone neither small nor delicate but in fact another man who is as mean as an Indian dog and a cheater who can shoot. You don't want a ballet dancer in there and Fast Fred Spokes was the best ballet dancer since the Russians took up the art. He also sweated a lot, a one-man irrigation system.

Fred grew up in Baltimore near the harbor, which has now all been fixed up into the kind of touristy place where they wouldn't let people like Fred grow up anymore. Being slender, he learned that the best way to avoid trouble was to stay away from collisions and Fast Fred Spokes was slick, I mean truly slick. He never is his life had more than two fouls in a game and he floated around, taking his exquisite shots from inside and outside the three-point line, untouched, like Dorian Gray, unscarred by the heavy duty business beneath the basket. Just grace. Amazing grace, but no defense.

"Hey, Coach," he would say when Big Jim talked about offensive rebounds, "just tell those big guys to pass off when they get tied up and I'll score. You don't need rebounds if you give the ball to the shooters." Fast Fred made $3,703.70 each time he walked onto the floor of a basketball arena. Fast Fred simply didn't want to fool around with the difficult business of rebounding and defense. The team was in disarray, like the Balkans before World War I. Raphael called Fast Fred "Rudolf," after the Russian ballet dancer.

There was talent among the big men but it just wasn't coalescing. At guard we were hurting. We only had one play maker, a guy named Isaiah Jones, a little six-footer, who had played at North Carolina State where he was a superstar and got a big contact from the Philadelphia Seventy-Sixers, but after his three years were up there they let him go to Denver where he got erratic, missing practices and once missing the plane on a road trip. Denver bounced him to San Diego, and the year before he'd come to Albuquerque as a back-up point guard. The starting point guard, Ham Fenson, had broken his foot in preseason, so Isaiah Jones was the starter, a classically good ball handler but as I say, erratic. He'd missed a couple of practices during our opening home stand and Big Jim Munson had fined him. Some nights Isaiah was a dream, feeding the ball into the thick of it with a wonderfully casual skill—other nights he spent the whole damn night dribbling around doing nothing. We were, simply, stuck with Isaiah since the rookie back-up was nowhere near experienced enough to play more than a few minutes a game.

The other starting guard, John Packer, whom the fans called Green Bay, was a totally ordinary talent: he could shoot fairly well, play defense fairly well, handle the ball fairly well, keep calm. He was six-six and large-boned, a product of Syracuse. Green Bay didn't say much, just plugged away at his mediocre game: a steady type, and we had no one better for his position.

So these were the six guys we really relied on: Raphael Flint, the aging grouch; Del Babbitt, the young and not awfully strong center; Fast Fred Spokes, the showboat; Mo Flynn, the gentle giant; Green Bay Packer, the boring guard; and Isaiah Jones, the seismically erratic playmaker. You'll meet the other guys later, but to go back to that night in December when we lost in Portland, I left the locker room feeling as beaten as the guys. We had to do something.

3 I DECIDED to walk the six blocks to Moriarity's and have a few beers and try to imagine how to turn these derelicts into a basketball team. I knew Big Jim was back in his hotel room having a bourbon and staring at the wall, wondering the same thing. Maybe the Irish music would give me an inspiration about Mo, I thought.

It was raining outside the arena, the kind of soft eternal rain you get in Portland, and there weren't very many people out on the streets. It was a Tuesday night and I speculated that no one who lives in Portland does anything on Tuesday nights. I was wrong and right. There weren't very many people in Moriarity's—a few couples in the booths and two guys at the bar looking forlorn. The band was taking a break.

I went down to the far end of the bar and took out a ten-dollar bill. The barkeep brought me a Harp beer in a big glass and I began to think of a crazy idea, the kind of idea that arises from desperation. Green Bay Packer, averaging five points a game, two rebounds and one assist, was simply not helping at all. We were stuck with Isaiah's mood shifts. The answer to the whole thing was Mo Flynn. If we could get Mo revved up we could put him in at small forward. Yeah! A six-eleven small forward. And we could put Fast Fred at shooting guard—he wasn't really quick enough but he might be able to adapt. Three huge guys up front.

Looking into my mug of Harp and seeing a new configuration on the basketball floor, I was vaguely aware that
someone had taken the next barstool. I went on with my
thoughts, mentally diagramming plays whereby Mo Flynn
would set the pick and Isaiah would bounce it to Fast Fred
who would duck around Mo and . . .

"It won't work."

I looked up and saw the quiet profile of a blond woman,
about twenty-five, I guessed. She was sitting to my left,
looking straight ahead.

"What did you say?" I asked.

"It won't work."

"What won't work?" I asked. I wondered if she was some
kind of a nut, having trouble with her marriage or her boy-
friend. She kept looking in front of her at the row of bottles ranged along the mirror. She was beautiful.

"Putting Spokes at guard," she said.

"How did you know I was thinking about that?"

She turned her face to me and smiled, a broad smile,
with a lightly lipsticked mouth.

"It would be the logical thing to think of," she said, "but
it won't work. Don't worry. I'm not a mindreader."

She was wearing a light brown suede jacket and a bright
pink blouse that looked like silk. Lots of ruffles around the
throat. On her right wrist was a big silver bracelet—Indian.
There was a silver and turquoise ring on her left hand. Her
blond hair hung straight down and I looked into her dark
sapphire eyes and felt as if the elevator had broken loose
and my innards were sinking. In a word, I was stunned.
Not just because this strange woman had apparently been
reading my mind, but because this strange woman was
without any qualification the most beautiful thing I had ever
seen in my entire life.

"Uh . . ." I said. And again: "Uh . . ."

"My name is Kendall Lea," she said, smiling slightly, as if she had some kind of joke in mind.

"I'm . . ."

"I know. Assistant coach of the Albuquerque Demons. Three and sixteen on the season. I can help you."

I looked at her and decided she was a nut. The most gorgeous nut in creation, but a nut.

"I'm sure I can help you."

"Uh, lady, listen, I mean what do you . . . how, uh, what is this?" I had a strange warm feeling in my stomach and suddenly the idea emerged in my brain that she *could* help us, God knows how. "Can I get you a drink?"

"Thank you. I'd like a Canadian whiskey on the rocks." I signaled the barkeep, who came over to our end of the bar and took the order, while I desperately tried to imagine what the hell I was going to say next.

"We've got our problems," I said.

"Yes, we do," she replied. *We?* I thought. "But they're solvable," she went on. "Think of them as challenges."

"Uh . . . what did you say your name was?"

"Kendall Lea. I'm from New York." She was looking at the bottles again. The barkeep slid up to us and put her Canadian whiskey down on the bar, withdrawing two dollars from my little pile. She was big-breasted, broad-shouldered. Her fingers were long—strong-looking. I was giddy and I didn't know what was happening, or what she was talking about. We?

"Are you here on some kind of business?" I asked.

"No," she said, turning her eyes on me again. "I flew out for the game."

"You flew out to Portland for a basketball game. What a fan."

"Well, I'm not actually a fan. In fact, I don't really follow basketball. It was only last week that I heard of the Albu-querque Demons, as a matter of fact, and so I flew out to Portland to see them play."

I took a sip of the Harp.

"Do you mind if I tell you that doesn't make any sense?"

"Oh," she said, laughing and my spine tingled at the sound of it. "It really does make sense. I'm a student."

"A student."

"Yes."

"Of what?"

"Well, you might say of human nature."

"So you flew three thousand miles to watch a last-place basketball team lose their sixteenth game. Sure, I see. That makes a whole lot of sense."

She laughed again, and I died at its wondrous glory, and considered asking her to marry me. She had to be crazy, but what the hell did I care? She was the only source of light in the world. I could imagine myself bringing her breakfast in bed, she sitting there propped against the pil-lows in my bedroom, a sapphire-studded wedding ring glinting in the morning light that comes through the east window, looking sleepy and soft like a cat that just woke up, smiling at my continuing thoughtfulness, admiring my powerful frame. . . .

She leaned forward, an elbow on the bar, and said: "It does sound a little odd, I know, but I truly do think I can help you and the team. It's a matter of knowing a few tech-niques."

"Techniques?" I said. I love this woman but she's some kind of arrogant. Between me and Jim Munson, we know all the techniques.

"The techniques of achieving human excellence," she said.

"Well, we sure as hell could use a little human excellence, I can tell you."

"Your team is surely good enough to get in the play-offs," she said, leaning slightly toward me. I could smell her perfume, very faint—my sense of smell is lousy—and I swooned twelve times. "All it takes is a little work on human excellence."

I don't care what blithering nonsense you say, I thought, I love you beyond dreaming, I'll follow you to the moon, I'll bring you an omlette on Mars. I'll learn to write sonnets.

"Well, see, I've been working on that myself and we've got a few hang-ups. The guys aren't working together. No one's sacrificing." Why, I thought, am I talking to this strange starlit woman about my profession? What the hell does she know? Only heard of the Demons last week? *I* know why I'm talking to this strange woman: because I don't want her ever to go away, I don't want her ever to be more than seven inches away from me.

"Well, you see, that's where I can help you," she said.

"How?"

"I'm a hypnotist."

A hypnotist, I thought. These guys are already playing in a trance. We need a HYPNOTIST? But I need this woman, I don't care what she is.

"It's a special kind of hypnotism. It's called neurolinguistics. Have you ever heard of it?"

"No, I don't think so. I don't get much of a chance to think about anything but basketball." This is crazy, I thought to myself. Maybe it's jet lag. Maybe I've got the flu.

"I was struck by the name of your team. The Demons. That's a word that's very important in neurolinguistics. What I do is to hypnotize people in a special way—actually there are a number of ways—and lead them back to a time when they were at their best. We call it a demon state. So," she laughed again and the earth leapt out of its orbit, "when I saw your team's name in the newspaper and saw how badly you were doing, I thought I should get on the plane and help you."

"Uh . . . we're going to Seattle tomorrow."

"Yes, I know. So am I."

Swoop. Leap. Sail. Fly on the wind, soar on the thermals.

"Maybe you better tell me about this stuff, this . . ."

"Neurolinguistics. It's kind of a mouthful, but it's really quite simple. And it works. For example, I can get that little man, what's his name? Isaiah Jones? I can get him off cocaine in about three sessions."

I gaped at her and she returned my gape with the calm, soft, beautiful glow of her exquisite eyes.

"How did you know he was on cocaine?" *I* knew he was on it and had started to talk to him about it. We had tiptoed around the subject for a week and he had finally admitted to me that he had the problem and we were going to look for help, but it seemed best to go slowly with him, so he wouldn't panic.

"It's perfectly obvious. And it's very sad. There's a terrible hole there somewhere in him and coke is how he fills it. I'll fill it with something that's better for him."

I stared at the bottles of Scotch, gleaming in rows.

"Like what?" I asked.

"His best."

His best. She said it like she was recommending aspirin, with all the assurance in the world. His best? I thought maybe I was dreaming.

"I'll take it," I said.

"Okay. When do we start?"

Start? Start? Tell Big Jim Munson I ran into this hypnotist in an Irish bar and I believe she can help us. Some kind of upper-crust groupie whom I have fallen in love with like the floodwaters of the Mississippi? I can hear Big Jim now: "Boy, you can't panic on me. This is a game of basics. What's this shit about linguistics?"

I took a sip of the Harp and leaned on an elbow.

"I have a question . . ." I said.

"The answer is maybe . . ." she said.

"When are we going to get married?" I asked.

"Maybe after the play-offs," she said. "That's what's important now."

I did the math. We were nineteen games into the season with another sixty-two to play before the play-offs which stretch on into late spring. I would have to wait until spring to collect this wondrous piece of work unto myself and hold it forever? Do you know how long a basketball season is? It's an outrage and I'll write the commissioner about shortening it. Too tough on the guys, the travel, the empty nights in strange cities, it all weirds people out, makes them think that some lady they met in an Irish pub in Portland is their wife-to-be. Turns a man to mush. I was mush.

"I love you," I said.

"We'll see," she replied with that smile that looked like there was a joke somewhere. "Meantime, let's get ourselves into the play-offs."

For the next hour and a half we talked, about the players and about words and symbols, and then I took Kendall Lea to her hotel which was a few blocks south and east of Moriarity's Irish Pub. At the door to the hotel, with a large and overweight man glowering at us from under his uniform cap, I took her by the elbow. Soar. Float.

"Can I ask you a question?"

"Later."

I walked back to my hotel in the rain and found myself taking jump shots at the lamp posts.

4 THE NEXT NIGHT OUT—in Seattle—we lost
again.

We made a nice run on those guys late in the
fourth quarter but it dried up. Raphael Flint broke
up a fast break with a superhuman block, practically driving the ball down the guy's throat, recovered it, and hurled
it down the court where Fast Fred dunked with an arrogance that made me tingle. Even Big Jim stood up from
the bench and clapped his big red hands. We got two more
hoops in a row, from fast Fred and from Green Bay Packer,
the latter being the result of a remarkable behind-the-back
pass from Isaiah Jones right into the traffic, and things were
looking good. But when, next time down court, Isaiah threw
it into the mob and they got it and the streak was dead.

Then Green Bay got hammered but was called for the
foul and Big Jim, now in a state of total frustration, said a
few bad things to Manny Rosenfield, who is one of the pris-
siest referees in the league, and picked up his second technical foul of the night, meaning he had to leave the arena
and meaning that I was in charge for the last few seconds.
After the foul shooting was over we were four points down.

"Mo," I said to the big redhead who was sitting next to
me on the bench. "Get in there, for Del, and when that
little guard sags on Raphael, I want you to get around him
on the left and stand there. Flex your knees. We need a
megapick. You got it?"

"I got it," said Mo, who hadn't really got it. Mo went in and tried to do what I had said and didn't and we lost. I tried to look calm as the guys schlepped off the court and I looked up through the lights into the crowd, trying to find Kendall Lea. Eventually I spotted her sitting alone in about the thirtieth row on the Seattle side. She was eating popcorn and reading a book.

I watched the guys slink off the court, watched the fans drift happily out of the arena—it had been one hell of an exciting game—and I looked again at Kendall Lea, still sitting there reading a book, and I picked up the six-foot long section of bench I'd been sitting on and threw it into the stands. It made a terrible crashing sound, startling the people who were leaving that bunch of seats, and it wound up costing me $750 in fines but I was glad I had done it. Kendall Lea looked up from her book, put her thumb and forefinger together in a circle, and winked.

My next job was to persuade Big Jim that he should listen to this golden angel.

The next day was an off-day. The guys lolled around the hotel in Seattle in their own private worlds. Big Jim and I sat in the coffee shop having lunch. I should have been nervous but I was feeling calm and smooth, despite my slightly red-rimmed eyes. I was still enjoying the morning's show. As arranged, Kendall Lea and I had met in the lobby of her hotel at nine-fifteen, had a cup of coffee, and went up to her room so I could get hypnotized.

There were a lot of books and papers strewn around on the little round table near the end of her bed. I looked at her hips as I followed her into the room. I wanted to put my hands on her hips.

"Well, what do I do?" I asked. "How does this work?"

She turned and said: "Just sit down and we'll talk for a

while." So I sat in one of the two little chairs and allowed myself to look into her dark eyes.

"The only thing you need now is to be comfortable sitting there," she said as she sat down across from me. "And we'll talk. And what will happen after a time is that your unconscious mind will come along and take over. Your unconscious mind has been taking care of you all your life, protecting your conscious mind from things you don't want to think about, doing its job beautifully, and when you go into a trance, the place I'm going to help you get to, your unconscious mind will be there to protect you and comfort you."

I looked into her eyes again. She had the beginnings of little lines around them. Laugh lines. Squint lines.

"You may find that you don't want to talk, but you will hear my voice. You're just going to take a journey. You'll go to a sweet place."

I looked at Kendall's splendid lap, then back to her eyes, and she blinked. I felt like warm sugar, like my body was beginning to give in to gravity.

"You may want to close your eyes, or you may want to keep them open."

She blinked again and I sank into the chair and it was as if the eye doctor had gently flipped another lens, creating a tunnel of pleasing dark beyond which lay the blue eyes and the smile lines and the eyes blinked again, or did they? And I heard her voice, soft, quiet say: "Yes, yes, it's a lovely place. You hear the traffic outside the hotel, but you're going to a beautiful quiet place. You feel better breathing more slowly. You see a beautiful place and you can smell it now and it's so quiet and the sun is warm on your face . . . and yes, that's a fire engine you hear outside the hotel but you're still among the trees . . ."

Her voice grew distant and my eyes closed and I smelled dawn among the spruces. I stared at the unimaginably tall tree before me, its boughs hanging down silent and strong. From far off a flicker called, a call of certitude and hope, and I heard her voice, so distant yet by my ear and I longed to say, "I love you," but I was silent like the valiant trees, so understanding of the needs of woodpeckers ·and soil and air. . . . Eventually I heard her voice say: ". . . and now, in your own time and your own way you will come back from the beautiful place you have found. You will go back there again anytime you choose. It is your place, a place where you will always know peace. And now, when you are ready, you will come back and your day will be fulfilled."

After a while—time had vanished—the cerulean sky over the spruce trees began to turn into a hotel room in Seattle and Kendall Lea was sitting before me, her face quiet, her dark eyes in repose, and I burst into tears.

Bursting into tears is not what your typical assistant coach in the NBA does, especially in the hotel room of the woman he knows only slightly but adores—it's not good for the image. But somehow, I felt maybe it wasn't so bad as I came back through gravity, sobbing and feeling somehow fulfilled. I knew, for example, Ellie wouldn't have liked living in a cabin either. Knew it for a fact.

"Excuse me," I hiccupped, wiping a drip from my nose.

"It's fine," she said.

"It was so beautiful, it just . . ."

"Yes, it can be surprisingly emotional. I'm glad it was beautiful. You looked very happy. It gets even better. There's a great deal you can do, and the best part of it is that you do it. I just help you get places—places in the world or places in time."

I looked at her eyes and the thought occurred to me that

even perfect gemstones can look trivial if you don't provide the perfect setting for them. The beginning of facial geology—the little lines—that was coming into being around her eyes astonished me.

"Kendall?"

"Yes?"

"I have decided something."

"What's that?"

"You are going to be the grandmother to my grandchildren."

She smiled.

"You do take the long view, don't you?" she said. "But we've got the play-offs to worry about now."

So in the coffee shop at one o'clock I was in a sense dreaming of spruce trees and other eternities when finally I broke a long silence between Big Jim and me and said:

"I may have run across something that will help us, Coach."

"You sure as hell didn't run across it last night in the fourth quarter," said Big Jim.

"Getting that technical there at the end didn't help much either," I said.

"I know that! God, this is frustrating. What the hell are we going to do, we've got to do something to get these guys together. The errors, the turnovers. They're too down even to have a practice."

"There's someone I'd like you to meet, Coach. Here in Seattle. It may sound goofy but listen. This person is what you call a human factors analyst. The problem with our guys is that they don't play together and each one of them has his own particular hang-up that keeps them from putting out 100 percent."

"You're telling me," said Big Jim, his big hand wrapped

around a bottle of Heineken. "You're telling me."

"Well, you see there's a technique for overcoming those hang-ups."

"Yeah, call off the season and send the whole bunch of 'em to a shrink."

"Something like that, actually," I said.

"Like what?" asked Big Jim, beginning to seem bored, probably his mind drifting off and making the same hopeless inventory of the talent on the Demons.

"Well, she says . . ."

"She?" Big Jim reddened. "This ain't girls' basketball." The coach was long and happily married to an old-fashioned woman about half his size who thought that the term chauvinist pig was probably some kind of French hog breed, and Big Jim didn't have much belief in the powers of women to do much but clean the house and raise babies. I knew, before I started, that I was in a lot of trouble, talking to Big Jim about Kendall Lea, and I had planned to talk more about her method before mentioning her gender. I'd slipped, and had probably lost the game.

"This is a highly trained scholar of neurolinguistics," I said. "Ever heard of it?"

"I don't think I could pronounce it."

"Well, I'd never heard of it till Portland when I ran into this lady, her name is Kendall Lea, and she's studied under three of the leading neurolinguistic types in the country, including the big ace, I forget his name, something like Grendel, in Santa Barbara. And she says that there are techniques for getting the guys to achieve personal human excellence. You know, live up to their potential."

"How?" said Big Jim with suspicion writ large on his brow. I knew he thought California was populated exclusively with flakes and an awesome enemy called the Lakers.

"Well, it's a kind of hypnosis."

Big Jim lurched and his bottle of Heineken dropped on the floor. "Goddamn it!" he said and reached down to pick up the bottle, still half full. "Goddamn it! These guys are already in a trance."

"That's just what I thought, Coach. When she told me, I thought the same thing. But . . . well, listen. Do me a favor. I know it sounds nutty but do me a favor and talk with her. Hell, we're going nowhere fast now, and I think . . . well, I think this lady might actually be able to help. What do we have to lose?"

"We could waste a lot of time," said Big Jim.

"This stuff is really different, Coach. Please, give it a try. Talk to her."

Big Jim looked at me like I was an insect, just stared at me until his eyes glazed over, and he was off somewhere else, rediagramming some maneuver or another. "Okay," he said eventually, his eyes still glazed. "Okay. Bring her around."

At four o'clock that afternoon I knocked on the door to Big Jim's room. At his bark, Kendall and I went in, to find him sitting like a block of stone in the little chair the hotel had provided. Kendall was dressed in a camel's hair suit, with a light blue cashmere sweater. Hanging on her chest was a gold pendant in the shape of a crescent moon. She walked toward the big man and I thought of lionesses, cheetahs.

"Mr. Munson, I'm so very happy we're having this opportunity to talk. The Demons are experiencing some difficulties and I'd like to talk to you about their successful resolution."

She put out her hand as Big Jim, remembering his old-fashioned manners in spite of his obvious discomfort, stood up from the ridiculous little chair.

"Yeah, pleased to meet you." He shook hands and sat down again. "So you've got the answer to this mess, huh?"

Kendall pulled another chair around, facing Big Jim and sat down, crossing her wonderful long thin legs. I noticed that she had big feet, narrow, with toes long enough to be prehensile. They were peeping out from a pair of fragile brown high heels with lots of little straps. I wanted to fall on the floor before them. Instead I sat on the bed and said: "Maybe you should kind of start from the beginning the way you did in Portland."

An hour and twenty minutes later, Big Jim Munson rose up from the little chair and came over to the bed. "Let me sit down." I moved aside and Big Jim settled on the bed, and picked up the receiver of the telephone. It looked absurdly small in his hand, like a kid's toy. He dialed a few numbers, mumbled "Room 309" and waited.

"Hello, Julia? Jim Munson. Is Mr. Bligh available?" Pause. "I know it was bad news. It's always bad news when you lose. We're trying our best with this gymful of no-hopers— basics, basics—but I have a new idea and I need to talk to Mr. Bligh about it." Pause. "Tub?" Pause. "Yeah, I know, I know. Look I've got a new idea. Yeah, something I think is going to work. It means I've got to add someone to the coaching staff."

There was a long pause during which the room was filled with the sound of a distant buzz saw.

"No, no, Tub. It's kind of an experiment. No salary for two months, and then if we get results, she only wants $2,000 a month and travel expenses."

The.buzz saw revved higher.

"Yeah, she's a she and she's a highly trained human factors analyst. She has a new technique for working with the guys. Getting them motivated."

Pause.

"No, it's not a new drug or anything like that, Tub. Look, trust me, will you? No, you're not going to be a laughing-stock. What the hell, we may even pick up some more fans. Yeah, we'll be the only team in the league with a female on the trainer's staff. Give it to the PR guys. They'll love it. Trust me, Tub. It can't cost us anything."

Yet another pause.

"Okay, Tub, see you in Albuquerque." He put down the phone and looked at Kendall Lea. He looked like a dopey golden retriever who had just gotten some confusing signal from his master. "You're on, Miss Lea. Welcome to the Demons."

Kendall Lea said thank you and smiled as though some remarkable joke was about to unfold.

5 ALBUQUERQUE, New Mexico, home of the Demons, then the least effective basketball team in the NBA, is a city without what you would call an idea behind it. It sits in a large shallow bowl of arid land, past which the Rio Grande flows without making much of an impression except to support a few bankside cottonwood trees, their roots reaching down for the vanishing moisture in the sand.

The city's roots go back to the time of the Spanish attempts to make America safe for Catholicism and the Crown—that is, some four hundred years ago—but most of Albuquerque looks like it was built within the last two weeks.

It's a lousy place to land in by airplane. The pilots like it because the runways are long and they can gun it, but for passengers it's like going to your first dance. Coming in, the planes hit the thermals caused by the Sandia Mountains that crouch to the east of the city and the planes lurch around like peas in a whistle and they give me the willies. I know they say it's takeoffs that are the dangerous maneuvers but landings freak me out: you know, all that tilting of wings and rearranging of speed and whatever. Takeoffs are like rockets—pure thrust—and they are easier on the mind, regardless of aerodynamics. Landings? Some loon or combination of loons landed a plane I was on in Albuquerque one night when the wind was blowing at 67 miles per hour and I thought I was going to turn into a jar of piss.

Once you've landed and relaxed, you've got more trouble. There doesn't seem to be a whole lot of logic to the naming of the streets and especially the freeways they built last night, all higgledy-piggledy over the streets. Another problem is that most of the city looks the same—vast stretches of two-story apartment complexes, fast-food joints, drive-in liquor stores, shopping centers, and other look-alikes. People showing up for the first time in Albuquerque usually get lost.

Actually I like the city. It's unpretentious. And the fans are great. A basketball town if there ever was one. Season tickets were sold out even though everyone in New Mexico knew the Demons would be abject losers. I like the Sandia Mountains rising up over the city and the worn-down remnants of volcanoes that punctuate the western horizon. I find the fast-food-hardware-booze drive-in combos comfortable. Nevertheless, it's a confusing cityscape for a newcomer and for that reason—and that reason alone—I devoted the next day to the task of showing Kendall Lea around.

"Are we anywhere near the university?" she asked, sitting beside me in the front seat of the Checker sedan I drive: headroom is everything if you're over six-four.

"Nope."

"Are there good places to live near the university?"

"Nope." She looked a little nervous. "Don't worry, there are some real nice places to live in Albuquerque." We were headed east towards the mountains, following the traffic up Candelaria Avenue, passing block after block of taco joints and clearance sales. Before long we started passing apartment buildings, two- and three-story places built to resemble Santa Fe.

"You'll love it," I said. A lot of Westchester County, New

York, was on her mind, I figured, green trees and intimate lawns. Albuquerque is not so amenable to the old English ideas of landscaping.

"It'll be okay," I said. "Don't be nervous."

"One of the things you're going to learn," she said, staring out the windshield, "is not to tell people not to be nervous. It makes them nervous. Lesson one from the human factors analyst."

She smiled.

"By the way," she went on, "where did you ever come up with that one?"

"I had a friend once, started a business, and needed a job description for someone whose job he couldn't explain to his board."

She smiled.

"What's the matter with the university area?" she asked.

"Central Avenue. Goes past the university. It's noisy. Guys cruise it all night. They've got their cars cranked down to an inch or two off the pavement and they go up and down at three miles an hour looking cool and traffic backs up to Bernalillo. You don't need that. It's bush league. It's like they're trying to be Los Angeles but lost the instruction book."

"The mountains are beautiful," she said.

"Most of the guys live out there, near the mountains."

"And I should live out near the guys?"

"I think so."

"So you live out near the mountains?"

"I live right here," I said and turned into El Camino Real apartments, a white-painted collection of stucco buildings, two stories high with wrought iron steps every ten feet or so. I crossed the tarmac welcoming mat and pulled into a

parking space that was marked with a red and yellow devil
on a plastic sign.

"Demon," I said.

"Got it," said Kendall Lea.

"I turned off the ignition."

"They think we're big stuff here."

"You will be," said Kendall Lea.

I fell in love again. I was getting used to the sensation of
falling, the little tickle somewhere down your throat as you
plummet into a sweet, all-enveloping fog. Warm.

She mounted the steps to the balcony from which my
door—stained dark and beaten with chains to make it look
like old timber—opened into a white living room. It had a
blue sofa and a matching chair, a coffee table that clearly
came from a department store sale, and a few posters of
Aspen in summer on the walls. It was sparse and stupid
and the most gorgeous woman on the planet had just entered
it.

"How beautiful," she said.

"What?" I asked. She strode across the living room and
looked through the sliding glass doors.

"The mountains. It's as if they were growing out of your
back door. Have you ever climbed up there?"

"No," I said, suddenly, feeling a seismic depression
descend. "See, we can find you a nice place, with a view of
the mountains . . ."

"This is fine."

"But . . ." I said, with Einsteinian wisdom.

"For a couple of months. I can use that spare bedroom
until we see if we can get the Demons in shape."

Now I ask you. I mean, I Ask You. The brightest star in
the firmament marches into my house and says "This is

fine"? She's going to live here? I will stagger into the kitchen in the morning for my breakfast of Coors and peanut butter and she will be in a terry cloth bathrobe saying would you like some bacon? I am expected to survive this?

"You've only got one problem," I said.

She looked at me questioningly.

"See, I happen to be in love with you and I don't know if I could stand having you around."

She looked up at me with the beginning of a grin on her face.

"I'm not sure I said that right," I said.

"Would . . . the guys . . . mind?"

"No, no, the guys don't care about . . . I mean, they don't, it's just, well, look, um."

"Then I don't see any problem. A couple of months maybe. I'll find a place later. We've got work to do."

I got her bags. We were scheduled for practice.

The arena is located in downtown, in just the right place to make traffic jams, but no one seems to mind. Near the locker room below the hardwood floor is a cement-block room painted yellow with chairs like classroom chairs and a blackboard. It was here that Big Jim Munson showed his diagrams to the guys, striding back and forth like some lobsterized geometry teacher, here that the guys, peering with varying degrees of comprehension, tried to imagine a way to translate a two-dimensional drawing into the sweat-soaked, muscular, and very three-dimensional world of basketball. They were sitting in the chairs, long legs askew, mostly wearing gray sweatshirts and sweatpants, wondering what the hell was going on.

There was a woman in the room. Their room.

Big Jim had called me at home and said he still wasn't sure why in the hell he had asked Kendall Lea to become part of the training staff and anyway he didn't know much about women. I had replied that he seemed to have stayed married to a woman for several decades, which was a lot better than I had done.

"Look," he had said, "never mind that. Liza's just my wife. I don't know anything about *women*. I don't know how to deal with this stuff. *You* know about women. You deal with this."

So it was my responsibility to introduce Kendall Lea to the team. Raphael Flint was sitting with his arms folded across his chest, a dark granite mountain in a bad mood. Isaiah Jones, the point guard, looked like a kid who is about to be told he's done something wrong—hooded, guarded. His eyes were bloodshot.

I was brief. I told them that Kendall Lea was a human factors analyst and had been hired by Jim Munson to serve on the training staff to work on group dynamics. The guys didn't have the faintest idea what I was talking about, and neither, of course, did I.

"She'll be working with all of us, individually and as a group. It's a highly experimental deal, a brand new idea in professional sports, and I want you all to give this a good chance. We aren't in a position to turn down a good idea, what with being last and all."

For a man his size, Raphael Flint has a surprisingly high and gentle voice. "Is she gonna come in the locker room, too?" he asked.

Kendall Lea stood up. She was wearing her bright pink blouse with the ruffles around her neck and a suede skirt. She smiled and her eyes crinkled up, sapphires dancing in a landscape of sincerity.

"Mr. Flint," she said, "I honestly believe that one of the most difficult things for a professional athlete—for people like you who are heroes to so many people—is privacy. I guarantee you that you'll never find me in the locker room."

Raphael looked skeptical and hunched his shoulders up.

"In fact," Kendall went on, "privacy is at the very center of my work. I practice what is called neurolinguistics." Mo Flynn the gentle, slightly intellectual giant, looked up, puzzlement on his face. "I work privately with individuals. Nobody knows what goes on between me and someone I'm working with. I don't even know."

She paused and the guys fidgeted around a bit, interested but confused. "You see, no one who works with me has to say anything to me at all. In fact, I doubt that anyone will feel like talking at all when we're working."

"Say, uh, just what's this working?" asked Raphael, looking highly suspicious. "You some kind of shrink? I don't need any *psycho*-analysis."

"No, I'm not a shrink," said Kendall Lea with a quiet smile. "I'm a kind of hypnotist."

"Hypnotist! Shee-it." This was Isaiah Jones.

"Isaiah, you watch your language around here." This was Big Jim.

"Sorry, coach."

Kendall turned to the coach and said: "That's really all right, Mr. Munson. I know all the words—or most of them—and I don't want anyone to do anything that's uncomfortable on account of me."

I had the sense that it had fallen apart. The game was over, the guys wouldn't play. There was nothing Kendall Lea could do now to get their confidence.

"Listen," said Kendall Lea, her voice soft and slow. "I'd like you all to relax about me. All I do is focus people's minds on their own excellence. We work in private. Part of it is just me talking. You men all know about basketball.

You're the jocks. I'm starting from scratch in basketball. I know this all seems nuts for now, but I'm itching to start and I know there are lots of ways I can help resolve some problems. For example, look at where your hands are now. Ten of you are scratching your balls. That's because I told you to." Mo Flynn grinned foolishly. Raphael Flint stared at the woman. There was a buzz, a lot of shifting of legs, a lot of confused men trying to look cool.

"What do you mean, you told us to?" asked Raphael.

"You see, Mr. Flint, most of what we all do every day is unconscious. Probably many of the things you do best in basketball you do unconsciously. You don't have to think about them with your conscious mind. You just do them when they're needed."

"Yeah, but so what?"

"Think back over what I said to you. You may remember that I emphasized certain words. Jocks. Itch. Ball. Nuts. And each time I said a word like that I made the same gesture . . . scratch." As she said the word she turned her hand over palm-upward, a simple gesture.

"That way I influenced your unconscious minds to do something you probably all wouldn't have done at the same time. Now I couldn't have gotten any of you to do something that would be harmful to you. Your unconscious mind protects you. It doesn't let you think about something that would be painful. I played that little trick so you could see what I do, see that it isn't anything scary or difficult."

Later at practice Raphael Flint came up to me, looking like he does when he fouls out of a game. He glared at me.

"Raphael, don't glare at me, man."

"Listen, what the hell was that? I still don't believe no woman can come in here and make us do things we don't want to."

"Well, look, Raphael, doesn't it seem like a pretty big coincidence that nine grown men all scratched their nuts at the same time in front of a strange woman who was looking right at them?"

"Well," said Raphael. "Two guys didn't."

"Okay, she's ten and two. We're three and eighteen."

Raphael looked uncomfortable.

"What else is she going to do?"

"I don't know, man, I really don't. That's between you and her. None of my business."

"Well, shit, man, this is some dip-assed way to run a basketball team." He turned and began to stride towards the opposite end of the court where the others were shooting lay-ups.

"Try it, Raphael," I called after him. "Big sonofabitch like you shouldn't be scared of a woman."

Raphael broke into a long-strided lope, took a pass and slammed the ball through the hoop so hard the backboard shook like jelly for ten seconds.

6 YOU KNOW HOW coaches tell the press that they just look as far down the road as the next game? "We're just thinking about Cleveland tomorrow night." That kind of crap? To some extent it's true, but no one who ever coached an NBA team ever went to bed without fretting about the entire rest of the season, the endless kaleidoscope of games and travel and injuries and screw-ups that are in store and how the hell, with the personnel at hand, the team is going to survive. Will so-and-so get his rhythm back? Will that hypochondriac asshole get over his tendonitis?

Well, the guys were so shaken by the sudden intervention of Kendall Lea in their midst that they didn't even concentrate on the game the next day—in fact, against Cleveland, another team most of the league beats up on regularly just like they did against us. Maybe they were so shocked at having a woman join the staff, or that the woman had made them involuntarily scratch their balls—or both—that they simply forgot their usual hang-ups. Anyway we won our fourth game of the season, 99–97. It was a sloppy game with a lot of fouls and the guys held on to the lead just long enough. Raphael hadn't done anything different but he did his usual things so ferociously that by the end of the game the Cleveland guys had been scared off him. I thought he was going to kill. Toward the end of the game, he was even getting room for his soft little turn-around jumper.

As we walked off the court, the fans going bananas—how many of them had seen a win this year?—I said to the coach: "Maybe it's an omen."

"There aren't omens in basketball," he growled. "Just basics."

After the practice the day before when the team had met Kendall Lea, I had asked her if she wanted to go to dinner. There wasn't anything to eat in the house anyway. We went to a Chinese restaurant on Juan Tabo Avenue (I have never thought to ask who the hell Juan Tabo was) that lies back in a shopping mall looking something like a warehouse. Once you're inside this place, called the China Hand, you wouldn't think it's going to be all that great—it looks a bit like a reconverted warehouse with vaguely Chinese decor that was obviously installed that same afternoon. But the food is usually first rate.

The captain, all smiles, bowing, led us to a booth along the wall, and left us the menu—all twelve volumes of it.

"Let's have a drink and some pot stickers first," I said. "Give us time to read this encyclopedia."

"Pot stickers?"

"You know, those little dumpling-type things, fried. All sorts of wonderful weird stuff inside."

"Oh, jao-tzes," said Kendall Lea. It sounded as if she had said "jounces."

"You're out in the West, honey. Low-down, earthy folks around here."

A diminutive waiter materialized at the table and we ordered jounces and scotch for me, Canadian whiskey for her. The drinks came immediately.

"Well, you sure pulled that one out," I said after the little waiter had glided off to deal with a brace of large blue-haired old women who were in apparent confusion at the next booth. Kendall smiled and looked off into some private distance. Her blond hair was down, brushing her shoulders, and I wanted worse than anything to touch her head.

"I mean, I thought it was all over when Big Jim was yelling at Isaiah about saying shit."

She turned. "Why is that?" she asked.

"Because the odds were about two million to one that the fact you are a woman was going to blow the deal in the first place. A basketball team is a pretty conservative men's club. Then Big Jim sort of widened the gap, you know, by suggesting you were a lady."

She looked at me with that smile like there's a joke.

"Well, you are, of course, you are a lady, but . . . you know what I mean."

"Yes."

"But you blew them out with that trick."

"Not all of them."

"Okay, so you're ten and two and you've just begun."

"Twelve and two. I got you and Mr. Munson. But some of the guys who responded to the trick aren't necessarily going to respond to anything else. Some of them will be tough."

"Mo?" I asked.

"He'll be easy. He's interested in it."

"Yeah, our intellectual teddy bear."

"Raphael will also be fairly easy, I think."

"Who then?" I asked.

"The little one, Isaiah Jones. He's a bit paranoid, like any addict, and he's surely thinking that there's some kind of conspiracy to get after him."

"There is," I said and she laughed and like the rest of the guys that night, I was too much mindful of Kendall Lea's presence on the club to think much about basketball. We agreed that she ought to start with the easiest one—the one who would show the most willingness and the most improvement the fastest. Mo Flynn.

The next day, the morning before our scraggly triumph over what the press calls the "hapless Cavaliers" (and they used more depressing adjectives about us), I had been trapped on my way into the arena by a little squirt about the size of a sixth-grader, a self-important little twerp named Dumfrey Schwartz. He's a smug member of a species of parasite known as sports columnists. All these guys are instant print versions of Howard Cosell, loudmouths running on for their own gratification without taking out a little time to find out what the hell they're talking about.

"I hear you've made some important changes in the coaching staff," he said in rapid-fire New Yorkese. He was wearing soft felt shoes and a corduroy jacket over a turtleneck T-shirt that clung loosely to his little neck.

"No, Dumfrey, no important changes to the coaching staff."

"Word is out that you've added someone," said Dumfrey.

"That's right. To the trainer's staff."

"A shrink."

"Not a shrink," I replied informatively.

"A woman."

"Correct. A woman. You can quote me, Dumfrey. Now I've got to get . . ."

"What can a woman do on a basketball team? I mean that's never happened before. This is big . . ."

"Dumfrey, it is not big. We have just added a woman to our professional training staff. She is a professional. Haven't you ever heard of women lawyers? Women doctors? Hell, you got a few women working on the *Journal*, don't you? Are you some kind of sexist, Dumfrey? The Demons are equal opportunity employers, you can quote me. Now buzz off." Dumfrey waddled off in his little felt shoes, the investigative reporter looking for a leak.

So the morning after we beat the Cavaliers, I was sitting in the kitchen with a can of Coors and a peanut butter sandwich, reading Dumfrey's column—which with nearly blinding creativity he calls *Today*.

> Could it be coincidence?
> They do happen, don't they?
> The ragtag Demons hung on in the stretch and beat back a surge from the hapless Cavs. It almost went down the tube but a few well-timed mental errors by Cleveland and some hard work under the boards kept the lead on the Demons' side of the scoreboard. And there were some great moments.
> Raphael Flint looked like the Raphael Flint of old, dominating the boards and unleashing his beautiful old jumper.
> Fast Fred Spokes streaked.
> But one has to wonder if this win didn't have something to do with a new arrival on the Demons' staff. A new "professional" named Kendall Lee [sic]. Kendall Lee is—hold onto your hats—a woman. . . .

On Dumfrey frothed, quoting "a player" as saying he didn't know what the new staffer's job was and didn't even remember her name. The front office had had nothing to say except that it was a routine addition to an overworked professional staff. Word had it that Big Jim Munson would discuss it all with the press in due time. A few more wild suggestions. "My guess is . . ." That sort of crap. Dumfrey Schwartz. I guess he's doing his job, but I wish they'd put someone in there who doesn't have to crane his neck to look at a basketball player's belt buckle. Little guys have just got to hate us.

Three important things happened that day. Kendall had her first session with Mo Flynn, we lost to the New York Knicks, and Kendall won the respect of Raphael Flint.

I was in a grouch about Dumfrey Schwartz, sitting in the kitchen with a second Coors, when Kendall Lea emerged into the kitchen and my grouch was over. She was dressed mostly in white—white cotton jeans and crêpe-paper-like shirt that looked ethnic, covering a light purple shirt underneath. Here and there were bits of turquoise. Her hair was up. The sun had risen in my kitchen.

"Want some breakfast?"

"I'd love one of those," she said, pointing at the beer.

"I've got eggs and bacon. Laid in real people's food yesterday."

She beamed and I fainted inside. "I try not to eat just before I work," she said. "Keeps the blood in my head, not my stomach." I fetched her a beer from the refrigerator and popped it open. It's a sound I love.

"Glass?"

"No. Listen, you don't have to wait on me."

"Kendall, for you, I would push a pencil to the moon with my nose. Let's get married."

She smiled and gulped down a little beer. "I do have to figure out a way to pull my own weight around here."

"What do you weigh?"

"One hundred and twenty-eight."

"I'm one-ninety so you relax. We've got to leave in a few minutes. Mo Flynn lives about fifteen minutes from here."

Heading down Tramway Boulevard in the Checker she sat quietly, looking to her right at the mountains. The morning sun was high enough behind them to make the crests glow yellow. In the evening at sunset they turn deep orange. The sky behind them was pure azure, not a cloud for a million miles. I figured she needed to concentrate or meditate or whatever the hell hypnotists do by way of warm-ups so I kept quiet and steered—I have cruise control among other amenities on my Checker.

"Do you remember the trance I put you in in Seattle?" she asked, still looking out the window.

"Forgot all of it," I said.

"That's all I'm going to do with Mo today. Just get him relaxed."

"Don't make him fall in love with you. I can't take competition. Makes me mean."

"I just want him to go to some nice place. Where did he grow up?"

"In New Jersey, I think. Near the ocean. He likes to go sailing but I don't see how they make sailboats big enough for him."

We drove the rest of the way in silence. Mo Flynn shares a place with Dell Babbit, the center, a small but high-ceil-inged house near the tramway that goes up the Sandias. They came to the Demons the same season. Their place is always a shambles except for the one day a week a Mexican cleaning lady comes in. Usually you can't trash a place that badly and keep the same cleaning lady very long, but this one, Maria or something, was so impressed by the idea of picking up after two local heroes that she even referred to them as "her boys" and usually found time to leave behind some Mexican dish for the two bottomless pits to gorge on.

We pulled up in front of the house.

"What time shall I pick you up?"

"Two hours okay?"

"Two hours."

I waited till Mo closed the door behind her and went off on an errand or two. I hate doing errands. Afterward, with an hour to go, I drove up to the window of a drive-in liquor store, bought a six-pack of Coors and put five in the cooler on the backseat. I pulled off Tramway Boulevard about a half mile from Mo's place and daydreamed until it was time to pick up our human factors analyst (HFA).

As she stepped into the car, long white-sheathed legs, and slid her hips onto the seat, I felt a tug somewhere in my diaphragm. Mo closed the door behind her and bent over to look in the window.

"Thanks, Kendall," he said, a smiling boyish mountain. "Hey, Coach, that was great. You ought to try it sometime."

"Right. See you at the arena, Mo."

We pulled out onto Tramway and headed home.

"Want a beer?"

"I'd love one."

I reached around behind me and extracted two, which she popped open, handing me one. I took it as a gesture of nearly total intimacy. After a few minutes I asked her, "Is it okay for me to ask how it went?"

"Beautifully, as far as I know. I explained it all to him and he went into his trance very easily. I'm pretty sure he was off sailing. He just sat there, breathing right and smiling. He's so big, sitting there like a red-haired Ferdinand the Bull."

"That's the bull that wouldn't fight?"

"Yes, he wanted to sit under the cork tree and smell the flowers."

"That's our Mo," I said. "What next?"

"I'm going to see if I can get him to find a time when he did fight and it was completely a good thing."

"What if he never did?" I asked.

She looked at me with that odd little smile.

"Then we'll use science fiction."

"What do you mean?"

"Mo's a reader. He's got a lot of books around, paperbacks. He's got the *Dune* trilogy. They're paperbacks but he's had them bound in hardcover. He'll find the hero to identify with in there."

I· hoped she wasn't a nut. It sounded nutty. I'd rather not have to spend my life with a nut.

That night the Demons sleepwalked through the first quarter, surged within two points by the end of the third. In the fourth period, Raphael ran out of steam, we were out-rebounded 14 to 3 and lost to the Knicks by sixteen points. Tub Bligh neither showed up in the locker room nor called and I thought our resident nut, the HFA, had better do something soon or next week Big Jim and I would be selling insurance somewhere.

After a bad home game Raphael Flint says nothing. To anyone. He showers, dresses, and slips out into the parking lot where he stands in the shadows while his wife, Dora, brings around the creamy white Chrysler, one of four large and expensive cars Raphael owns. They live in a big house where the Sandias rise up. The house has a high wall around it.

After the loss to the Knicks, I went out to the parking lot with Kendall Lea. The blue light from the lampposts made huge nauseous circles of brightness. I noticed a large shape in the shadows over near Lot B. That was Raphael. I wondered where his wife was. Then a small figure waddled up to Raphael, looking washed out in the blue light, frail as it moved into the shadows.

"We better get over there," I told Kendall. "It's that asshole Schwartz and he could get killed if he pulls his usual routine."

When we got into earshot, we could hear Schwartz's nasal,

insistent voice: ". . . looks like you ran out of steam there in the fourth. Too bad. Maybe you're getting a little long in the tooth for this racket. It's a long season and . . ."

There was a growl from Raphael and Kendall strode up to them, a few steps ahead of me.

"You must be Dumfrey Schwartz," she said, enthusiastically. "I'm Kendall Lea." She stuck out her hand and Dumfrey, a little startled, reached out automatically to shake hands, and the most extraordinary thing I've ever seen happened. Just before their two hands met, Kendall's left hand darted out, grabbed Schwartz's extended right wrist, and yanked his arm up over his head, and held it there.

"You're not going to remember what I say in your conscious mind," Kendall said in a clipped, almost hurried voice. "From now on you are going to find rewards in being more sensitive in the way you greet the human beings you interview. You will consider each person you interview with the good will you would like to receive from others. Your private pains will no longer keep you from this rewarding new style and your column will become the best in the paper.

"Now, when I release you from this trance, you will giggle, scratch your head, and leave immediately."

She let his arm drop, and shook his hand. Dumfrey stood glazed like a ceramic pot.

Kendall smiled dazzlingly, and said: "It's so nice to meet someone who's normal-sized around here. These guys are all so big my neck hurts from staring up."

Dumfrey, eyes darting back and forth, giggled nasally, and scratched his head.

"Yeah, I'll talk to you later. I've got a deadline to meet." He turned and scuttled out into the light, narrowly missing impact with Raphael's big white Chrysler, now approaching with a quiet purr.

"What the hell was that?" said Raphael in his surprisingly high voice.

"I put him in a trance. If you interrupt an automatic behavior like shaking hands, you can put someone under immediately. He won't remember but I think you'll see a difference in his column."

The window of the Chrysler rolled down and a round brown face was visible in the shadows.

"Raphael? Sorry I'm late. Doggone car flooded."

"Never mind," said Raphael, and turned to me. "Does that stuff work?"

I shrugged. "Looks like it."

Raphael stood still as a boulder for what seemed ten seconds.

"Dora," he said, "you get out of the car. I want you to meet the new member of the Demons' staff."

7 MY OFFICE, generously afforded me by the Albuquerque Demons management, is an eight-by-eight
cinderblock cell with yellow walls and a desk of gray
metal and plastic on top of which is a phone by
which no one ever calls to ask me to be head coach of an
NBA team. Face it, an assistant coach doesn't need an office.
He needs a Ph.D. in psychology. I was sitting there the
morning after Kendall Lea had put that little twerp from
the *Journal* in a trance. Dumfrey had not said ragtag once
in describing our loss to the Knicks. He hadn't mentioned
Raphael Flint, either, talking mostly about Fast Fred's
shooting—which in fact hadn't been that much of a factor
one way or the other.

There appeared at the door a lithe, young-looking forty-
year-old, boyishly handsome and bedecked in $600 cowboy
boots, a pin-striped gray suit and a crooked grin.

"Hi, Taxbreak," I said. "Come on in."

It was Albert Dietweiler, M.D.

Dietweiler is the leading orthopedic surgeon in Albuquerque, a professor of physical anthropology at the university, and the Demons' team doctor, for which he is paid
a pittance relative to normal doctors' fees. He is a millionaire and we call him Taxbreak because, what with his ranch
about forty miles south towards Truth or Consequences,
N.M., where he has a couple of quarter-million-dollar
quarter horses dispensing sperm every day at an accoun-

tant's loss, he hasn't paid a dime to Uncle Sam since he was three years out of medical school, if then.

"Hey, I hear you hired a new trainer," he said, sliding elegantly into the metal chair before my desk.

"Yup."

"I read about it in the papers," said Taxbreak, with his charming and often phoney smile. "Dumfrey says she's a shrink."

"Dumfrey needs his head replaced," I said.

"I can do that. Hips. Knees. I can replace anything."

"Actually," I said, "I think it's already been done."

Not understanding, Taxbreak laughed, a fluid, rippling sound. "So tell me about the new addition."

"She's a human factors analyst."

"Hey, hey, that's terrific," said Taxbreak. "Just what the team needs." He leaned forward conspiratorially and whispered: "What's a human factors analyst?"

I leaned forward and whispered back: "Beats me."

"So what has she done?"

"Well, so far she got nine of the guys to scratch their balls simultaneously by just talking to them."

The doctor burst into laughter.

"A *hypnotist*," he gasped. "You mean you guys hired a fucking hypnotist? Marvelous, marvelous. Can I meet her?"

I picked up the phone and punched out an extension number. A few minutes later, Kendall appeared in the doorway and Taxbreak leapt alertly to his feet, his smile charming.

"Hi, I'm Albert Dietweiler, team doctor. Welcome to the staff." Smooth as oil on an Arkansas sharpening stone. "I heard you're an acupuncturist," Taxbreak went on with a big grin. "You'll have to be careful. These guys have such illusions about the size of their peckers, they won't let you go anywhere above their knees with a needle." Taxbreak guffawed at his own joke.

Kendall smiled that smile and I knew something was coming straight from left field.

"Glad to meet you, doctor," she said. "Yes, I can do acupuncture, but when I work on their knees there won't be any problem at all."

She paused.

"All they'll be worried about then," she went on, "is their solar plexus."

"How's that," asked Taxbreak with his movie-star anticipatory smile.

"I'll strip first."

You would have thought Taxbreak was going to die.

"Oh gross me out, megarepulsive," he gasped, slapping his well-tailored thigh. "Oh, beautiful! I love it." While Taxbreak was cackling, his long-lashed eyes wet with tears, I glanced over at Kendall Lea and noticed she was blushing. What the hell is a nice girl doing in a place like this, I thought to myself. Taxbreak coughed to a stop.

"Seriously," he said, "I know a little bit about hypnosis. I'd like to talk to you about this team."

She glanced at me and I nodded. Dietweiler was a millionaire, nouveau riche like the rest of us, and he wanted to be one of the boys, but when it came to actual medical stuff, he was all business, the best in the Southwest. Kendall and Taxbreak left for her cubicle.

The human knee did not evolve as a device for withstanding the punishment the NBA and owners of other coliseums provide by putting freaks—it used to be Christians—out to perform. Knees are delicate—the same sort of component as the arm on a record turntable, the fragile place where Murphy's Law operates first. Another place is the back. We invented basketball too soon. The knees can't take it and the human back never got far enough along to be completely upright. Add a lot of weight and you've got engineering problems, especially after the enthusiastic and youthful muscles surrounding the cartilage and bone in these danger zones begin to lose their youth and enthusiasm. That's why you hire a good doctor for a professional sports team. Not good in the hippocratic sense—some doctors are into preventative medicine these days which, if enforced, would put the NBA out of business—but good in repairs. Patchwork. Keep the freaks moving somehow. That's Taxbreak's job, along with the training staff, the guys who administer whirlpool baths, ice, heat, poultices, salves, exercise, and sometimes—well, hell, lots of times—one or another kind of dope to the ever more gelatinous bits and pieces of bone and cartilage that get crunched on the hardwood floors eighty-one nights a year. I got out after four years and I still can't do deep kneebends.

I wondered what Taxbreak would learn from Kendall Lea. How to hypnotize an anterior cruciate tendon in a knee?

We were a quarter of the way through the season almost. Four and eighteen and in last place. Our starting point guard, our play maker, was out with a long-term injury. His replacement, Isaiah Jones, was on cocaine. Our power forward was running out of steam, as Dumfrey had put it with accuracy. Furthermore our power forward was playing only for himself. Our center was a reed, our small forward a showboat who didn't want to get dirty, and the shooting guard—Green Bay Packer—was a bore. Mo Flynn, our sixth man? I hoped Kendall Lea would find him his hero—I didn't care if she had to have the sonofabitch airmailed from Alpha Centuri. Collect.

Big Jim had looked apoplectic after we lost to the Knicks.

Too red. The guy is going to kill himself if he keeps getting so emotional and internal. He should try throwing the bench into the stands a few times. It clears out the sinuses and costs you only $750 for a first offense. Maybe Kendall Lea ought to hypnotize the old lion, get him to relax. Can you imagine? Maybe she'll make Mo Flynn a killer and get Isaiah off coke and we'll rally and eke into the play-offs. And maybe she's a nut and we're doomed to rehearsing basics and to last place.

Somewhere I read once that they call reveries like that brown studies but in the NBA you watch your color metaphors. A very dark brown study in determination darkened the door to my little yellow cubicle. Raphael Flint stepped in and lowered himself into the chair.

"Hey," he said, nearly glaring. I don't think I had ever seen Raphael smile. It's either glare or near-glare. "I don't understand why a business that runs a basketball team can't put a few chairs around that fit a normal-sized basketball player."

Raphael was in a good mood.

"This place ain't even big enough for you," he added.

He looked around at nothing in particular.

"Dip-ass office you got here," he commented. I looked at him. "What you need, boy, is a big office with a window behindjue and a big desk made out some kind of teek or mahgony, give you a little authority."

"I didn't know you were from the South," I said.

Raphael snorted.

"What's on your mind, Raphael?" I asked.

"I want to see the shrink."

"She's not a shrink, she's a human factors analyst."

"Never mind all that crap. When do I get to see her?"

"What do you want to see her about, Raphael?" I asked.

"I want to find out a little bit about that number she run on the Flit. If I could do that to some of those guys—you know, out there at the beginning of the game, talk a little to the jerk who's on me—well, shit, man, put 'em out of business."

He was serious.

"Raphael, you got other ways of putting 'em out of business.

Raphael glowered. "You bet your ass I do. But I ain't such an old dowg I can't learn no new tricks."

"I really *didn't* know you came from the south."

"So when do I get to see her?" the big man asked.

"Hell, anytime you want. She's down the hall. She's talking to Taxbreak right now. By the way, how are your knees today?"

"Nothin wrong with my knees, boy. Made of whipcord and steel. I want to learn that trick with the handshaking stuff. I'll go down and get that smart-ass doctor out of there. I want to learn that trick." He began to rise from the little chair.

"Well, Raphael," I said. "Maybe you ought to give her a little time. Right now she's started to work with Mo, you know, trying to get him motivated . . ."

"That rabbit? Motivated to do what?"

"Come on, Raphael."

"Look," said Raphael, now standing and looking down at me with the authority of some ancient African deity. "I," he said, "I happen to be a starter. Mo Flynn is the sixth man around here. Six." He stuck out his enormous hand, fingers extended. "You don't count him on one hand. See you, boy." Raphael left by eight-by-eight cubicle and I thought again, what's a nice girl like you doing in a place like this?

We were hanging by the slenderest of threads, to coin a term, a young aristocrat from Westchester County who had gone to some snooty damn school which her father gratefully shelled out the cash for and who then went into fruitcake full time, learning how to hypnotize people—and acupuncture, too?—and then joined a basketball team, a bunch of bunheads playing a boy's game in front of ravening fans, getting written up in the newspapers on the sports page as being some kind of mysterious and inappropriate presence and I wondered what her old man must be thinking now. It was a long time, in fact, before I did find out what her old man was thinking and the days passed and the season wore on and, believe it or not, we played .500 ball for a week and a half, part of it on the road.

Kendall Lea found Mo Flynn's hero. She had tried to take Mo back into a time when he was a little kid and had rescued someone from a big problem with the big kids or something like that but either Mo had never done anything like that or, when he had, it had scared him. They roved around in Mo's past for two sessions and came up with nothing but Ferdinand the Bull, loving peace and fearing the infliction of hurt, neither of which have anything to do with basketball. So it was science fiction. The *Dune* trilogy, a bunch of weirdo books about a planet that's all desert and inhabited by giant worms, run by a royal family, and all hell breaks loose and the family leader of the time learns to apply force properly to win the planet back from the invading hordes. They made a movie about it recently which was so full of special effects that it was incomprehensible to everyone but twelve-year olds. After Kendall Lea's third session, Mo began to affect silver jeans like something out of *Star Trek* and Kendall said to me one night over a steak in some one of the steak houses that are sprinkled around Albuquerque like pepper—she said: "You've got Mo. Give him more minutes, gradually."

By then, see, Kendall had learned the business about minutes—how long you play in each game. All the players keep a mental if not actual record of how many minutes they play, average it out, and use it either to increase the financial burden they intend to place on the owner next season or to determine when they should get traded. Agents receive these statistics into contract-writing computers and in the off-season it's computer against computer. Whoever the guy was who invented basketball, he probably never dreamed about computers and agents. I don't, either. That's the general manager's job, and Tub Bligh has made the mistake of thinking he can be his own general manager and sell molybdenum as well. I dream about Kendall Lea and a ball made of petrochemicals dropping through a hoop that is a bit more than a foot in diameter with a sound like a brief sigh of the wind.

Anyway, Kendall Lea had reminded the team intellec-tual of his hero on the planet Dune and we gave him more minutes. The first night out, after Kendall gave us the go ahead, Mo fouled out in twenty-one minutes but the car-nage was enough to warm the cockles of your heart. One very dangerous forward on the Milwaukee Bucks was out for three weeks with a thigh that looked like one of the hot-air balloons they like to fly over Albuquerque. Several other players had learned a lot of respect in other ways not so obvious. We won that one, and Milwaukee was tough, obvious play-off contenders.

It went on like that for four more games. Mo going in at certain points and terrorizing the court and fouling out, wandering off the court with a silly Irish grin on his face. And we were playing .500 ball, winning half our games, still way behind in the league, but .500 for the time that Kendall had been with us.

"We've got to do something about Mo," I said one night in my apartment when we were sitting up a little late, having a nightcap of scotch. We'd run out of Canadian whiskey. "He's so clumsy out there now he's not doing what he could."

"I don't do delicacy. I do motivation."

That's what this magnificent collection of life and matter said to me in my own living room, which by then she had bedecked with five asparagus ferns. She smiled.

"Send him to ballet school."

"You've been talking with Raphael, right?"

"Right," she said. "I'm meeting with Raphael tomorrow."

It was raining. It doesn't rain that much in Albuquerque and the sound of the water dripping off the Santa Fe–type roof, pouring through a pipe so that it would hit the ground a few feet away from the walls, was unfamiliar, disconcerting. Kendall Lea was wearing a pair of white jeans, her long thin feet bare, and she was sitting in the easy chair, her legs drawn up. A strand of blond hair hung past her eye.

"We should talk about Raphael from your standpoint," she said.

"My standpoint?"

"Basics. What's the problem?"

She bent her big toe around the next one (thinner and longer) and cracked it.

"I love you," I said. "That's the problem."

"I love you, too," she said and all of New Mexico vanished into a crevasse. My heartbeat quadrupled and I felt like a great weight, something akin to a large apartment building, was sitting on my chest. I think I turned blue.

"Are you okay?" Kendall asked in her quizzical way.

"I think I died. What did you say?"

"I said I love you, too."

"Holy shit."

Kendall Lea smiled, peering out over her knees.

"That's what I seem to say when something surprising happens," I said.

She put her long-toed bare feet on the carpet and stood up. "I'll get the lights," she said and clicked off the standing lamp behind her chair. Like a slow-motion flood tide she moved across the carpet into the little kitchen and, blink, that light went off. All the lights went off in my apartment and all the lights went on that night—all the lights that ever shone in the universe since the Big Bang or whatever the hell it is that made this marvelous place. Every color and every intensity, flashing lights, purple and green, like Las Vegas was a first draft, New York City a sixth-grade book report. Lights? There's never been a kaleidoscope like it, ever before or ever since.

I woke up thinking about how we needed a new calendar—all that B.C. stuff and A.D. stuff was superannuated—and realized my head was buried in the sweet armpit of Kendall Lea.

It was still raining and the sound reminded me that I had to pee.

"Holy shit," I said.

There was a shift in the bed. She pushed her hair from her eyes like a little girl, a clumsy kind of gesture, and said: "*Now* what's so surprising?"

"It just struck me," I said, "that I am lying here in Albuquerque, New Mexico, U.S.A., Solar System, Universe, with my nose in your ribs. I'm very happy. I have to pee."

"So do I."

"Should I get you your bathrobe?"

"Give it to the Goodwill people," she said and went "mmmm" and fell asleep again. Noblesse oblige. I did my chores and returned in about twenty minutes with a platter of bacon and eggs, orange juice, and two cans of Coors.

"You look nice," she said. "Sort of like a race horse."

"So do you," I said, as she sat up and contemplated the platter.

"I think I'm very happy to be here," she said in a sleepy voice.

"That makes two of us."

She picked up a piece of bacon and looked at it like some strange mollusk. Then she munched down its length.

"I definitely am very happy here," she said. "Tell me about Raphael Flint."

You have to understand that I was standing in the door, leaning against the door jamb, having cooked a little breakfast for a woman that would put Helen of Troy in the category of also-ran, naked she was, sitting in my bed munching on bacon I had cooked with great care, and reaching for a Coors beer, its golden exterior like a dull rock when compared to the beauty of the creature in my bed, and I was asked to discuss Raphael Flint.

I coughed. I cough a lot in the morning because I am allergic to beer but I'd rather have a few beers and cough in the morning. It's good for the abdominal muscles.

"Well," I said, as I stopped coughing. "Raphael is a superstar. He's selfish. He plays only his own game. He makes twenty-five trillion dollars a year and no one tells him what to do. He wants the record for points scored, and he won't get it, and he wants the record for blocked shots and he won't get that, either. But he's close. He wants to be traded."

"He's a very nice man," said Kendall Lea.

"Most people don't think so," I answered. Kendall Lea devoured another rasher of bacon and pulled on the Coors.

"He's from Detroit?" she asked.

"The worst part of Detroit," I said. "And at the worst time. I imagine he was part of those gangs as a kid. The ones that sacked the place. A lot of rough stuff."

Kendall put the tray aside and lay back on the pillow, pulling the sheet up, to my utter dismay. "He really is a very nice man," she said. "I asked him a few questions and he looked up." She rolled her eyes up. "He is really very simple, very inexperienced. Naive."

"Hey, Kendall, we're going to have to make a deal here." Her blue eyes swiveled toward me. I sat on the bed and she moved her foot to touch me under the blanket. "See, I know that what you're doing is private so I won't ask you about it. And you don't have to tell me what you do with the guys. And I won't ask them. You're the motivator now. Me and Big Jim are just here to work out strategy and tactics on the floor. And basics. What I mean is I don't really know what you're doing and that's okay. What I really want is to be able to wake up in the same place tomorrow. I love you more than termites like wood."

She reached out with one hand and the sheet dropped and I seem to recall her saying something like "Thank you. Thank you for your love and thank you for your trust." The sun was up, I know that, but it turned purple in the room.

Later that day I asked Kendall Lea when I would get my next trance. We were in the Checker headed west to the arena, waiting for a traffic light to change. A huge truck pulled up beside us, roaring stridently.

She put her hand on my arm, leaning over, and said: "You should wait. It's the guys who need help. You're whole."

I stalled the car, right in the middle of the goddamned intersection.

8 IT HAPPENED AGAIN. The miracle, I mean. I woke up in the same place as the day before, with my head in Kendall Lea's armpit, my nose in her ribs. I could feel her rhythmic breathing. She was awake.

I opened my eyes and peered over the curve of flesh. Her eyes were open, looking at the ceiling. She glanced at me.

"Hi," she said.

"High as a kite, in fact."

She smiled. "Pretty good for seven o'clock in the morning."

"Seven? What are we doing up at seven?" I asked.

"We're not up," she answered. "We're in bed."

Dreamily, I watched the clouds scud by across the top of the stucco wall outside the window. I noticed that if you didn't concentrate too much and looked at the edge of the wall out of the side of your eye, it looked like the wall was moving, not the clouds. An illusion.

"This isn't a dream, is it?" I asked.

"What isn't?"

"You. Here." I answered.

She rolled over on her side, facing me and kissed me on my left eye. "Did you ever hear of Bishop Berkeley? He was an English philosopher who said that nothing was real. Everything was simply an illusion, a product of the eye and the mind. Then a guy named Samuel Johnson came along and kicked a rock across the street and said something like 'So much for Bishop Berkeley.' "

"And you just kissed me on the eye."

"Right. It was me."

"Fuck Bishop Berkeley. Go, Sam," I said and went back to sleep. I woke up some time later to the smell of bacon. In a few minutes, Kendall Lea came in the room bearing a tray.

"Tit for tat," she said. "Your turn for breakfast in bed."

"I ain't got no tats," I said.

"You're a real card," she said and set the tray down on the bed. She was wearing an apron. An apron that some barbecue restaurant had made up special with the team's name on it—DEMONS—and the M was a devil's fork the way it is on our uniforms. They'd given them to everyone on the team and I had put mine away somewhere and never used it because I don't cook barbecue and I don't wear aprons anyway. But Kendall Lea had on the apron. That was all she had on and it looked nice.

She sat on the bed while I began munching. "Yesterday," she said, "you told me I didn't have to let you know what I was doing with the guys, what happened when we met and all that."

She paused and I looked down her apron.

"Did you mean you really don't want to know or just that you don't need to?"

"I meant that I trust you," I said.

"But would you like to know?"

"Sure," I said, "but you know, you're sort of like a doctor and I don't want to violate whatever that code is between doctors and patients."

"Well," she said laughingly, "I'm not really a doctor, and

I am on your staff—and well, doesn't that orthopod tell you what the X rays say? Anyway, I need to talk about this stuff."

"So tell me about Raphael," I said.

It seems that Kendall Lea had arrived at Raphael's secluded place about the same time that Raphael's kid, Darrel, got there after school. The kid, who was about twelve, had introduced himself and Kendall had been charmed. Apparently it went in both directions. They had walked into the house together.

"Hey, Mom," Darrel had said, "This is my friend, Kendall."

After that, Kendall Lea explained, it was a piece of cake. Raphael wasn't there—off on an errand—and Dora had ushered her into the long, low house and offered her something to drink.

"It turns out to be pretty simple," said Kendall Lea. "Raphael's problem."

"Simple?"

"Yes, it goes back to one event, basically. He was part of a gang in Detroit. They called themselves something like the Black Tide and like all of those gangs, they had their territory where they literally ran the place even though they were mostly teen-agers. Raphael was one of the youngest in the gang, but his size was, well, exceptional even then.

"There is a bond of loyalty among gang members which is very strong and very essential. They broke it."

"What do you mean?" I asked.

"There was some trouble, some kind of rumble with another gang, and it spilled over. Some bystanders were hurt. The gang was in big trouble so they let the cops take Raphael. Just threw him to the wolves. He got a suspended sentence for assault and was on parole for two years. Did you know he had a record?"

"No."

"Well, Raphael simply hasn't trusted anyone ever since. He's a loner by way of self-protection."

I got up and fetched a Coors from the kitchen. "So what do we do about that?"

"Find another time, before that, when he took great comfort and got some advantage from a group."

"Like what," I asked.

"I don't know," said Kendall Lea. "But he'll find it."

It was about noon that same day and we were headed back from the arena. The Sandias were what you'd call a purple brown, dusted with the palest blue powdered snow, like some sort of dessert. The sun was low but strong as it always is in Albuquerque even in winter. We were now into late January and the Demons were playing better than .500. Days were coming up sharp and clear and clean.

Here in Albuquerque, the sun is strong all year. If you're out of the shadow in winter, you can wear a T-shirt. If you're really hot here in summer, you can step into the shade and it drops 15 degrees. That's because it's dry. There are no little microscopic bubbles of moisture around to carry the heat—or the cold—around the corner. The sun is warm. The shade is cool. This is a lot more civilized than a lot of places, regardless of their cultural installations. I'd trade lack of humidity for fifteen Lincoln Centers in New York.

Anyway, Kendall Lea and I were heading toward the snow-dusted Sandias and home after a morning at the arena, with four days off. No games. It was the All-Star break and no one had thought to select an Albuquerque Demon as an All-Star.

"Why don't we let 'em relax," Big Jim had said, "before we go west."

So Kendall and I were breezing along in the Checker and she said, "You know, speaking of tits for tats, I probably ought to rent a car, or buy one."

"Why?"

"Well, in a sense I like being squired around but it does make me a little dependent on you and—what I really mean is that maybe you shouldn't have to—I mean, maybe you shouldn't have to adjust your schedule to mine—or vice-versa."

"Yeah, okay, I see what you mean," I said. "Let's look into it. Tomorrow."

She looked at me in a strange way. Her eyebrows were raised and her mouth a bit tight.

"I mean," I said, "why shouldn't you be free to move around? You know, I'm perfectly happy to run you around but you probably ought to have the freedom to get around by yourself."

She looked at me with an even more strange look.

"You don't love me," she said and burst into an exaggerated set of tears. "Oh, my God, after all I've done for you, you want me to go off on my own."

She then burst into laughter and I was sufficiently distracted to run a red light for which I was paid by some asshole's horn.

"Listen, hypnotist, don't run your numbers on me," I said.

We drove on in a comfortable silence, and I wondered how it could be possible that I was happy with someone who could play linguistic games with me any time she chose and I would never know if it was a game or if it was serious. How did anyone ever get happy with someone else in a permanent sort of way? A conundrum, of course, to which no one has ever known an answer. Maybe it's like knowing that when you drive into the middle of a bunch of basketball players around the basket and the guys on your team know that when you do it a certain way you're going to be in the right place and they give you the ball and it works. Trust. I'd played a fair amount of basketball and otherwise been a loner most of my life and I had no right to give myself the luxury of trusting very many people but I simply trusted Kendall Lea with my personality. She wasn't a cheater. I knew that better than anybody. It was okay.

We pulled into the apartment complex and outside my place there was the goddamnest-looking car you could imagine. Or at least the goddamnest car I could imagine. It was a Cadillac. Vintage, you'd say, about a 1959—a boat. It was glistening with shiny lilac paint—a real pale lilac. The top was down even though it was late January. The rear license plate said DEMONS. The seat covers were white and they were fitted with sheepskins.

"Good lord!" Kendall said. "What's that?"

"Looks like a Cadillac," I said.

"Whose is it?" Kendall said. "It's the most amazing thing I've ever seen."

"Well, I've never seen it before," I said. "Let's take a look." I walked over to the passenger side and opened the glove compartment. Inside I felt a plastic envelope which I took out and opened, fumbling some papers out of it. I peered at the papers and said: "It seems to be registered in the name of someone named Kendall Lea. I guess it's yours."

Kendall Lea was standing by the Checker in her white slacks and shirt and her bright little Guatemalan belt. Her face went through the moves of a kaleidoscope, her eyebrow leapt up and down and she shifted from leg to leg twelve times in a second or two, making her hips swivel like the chimes on a clock.

"You . . ." she said. Her hand went to her neck. "You . . ."

"Happy birthday," I said.

She was still gasping in her throat. "How did you know it was my birthday?"

"I got friends in personnel. I checked out the papers you filled out. The car was born the same year as you."

"How," she glugged. "How did you know that color is my . . ."

"I guessed."

Kendall Lea weighs about 130 pounds and she placed all of them in the air and sailed at me, slamming me against the side of the Cadillac.

"Hey, look, we don't want dents in your car," I said. "Want to try it out?" I fished in the plastic envelope and pulled out the keys.

"I want to feel it first," she said, poking her head over the seats like a stork peering into a nest. "What's this?"

"Well, that's a Coleman cooler," I said. "It's full."

She reached into the back seat and opened it up. The bottle of champagne was on top of the ice. Below was a sixpack of Coors.

"I thought we might drive down to Truth or Consequences and look in on Taxbreak."

Kendall Lea is one of the strongest women I've ever met. I thought I'd gotten a broken rib. Well, at least, I thought, Taxbreak can tell me what to do about it.

Kendall Lea poked around the car, touching things and saying "ohhh." She then turned around and walked toward me, her long legs striding in a way that most women can't move—a cross between feminine sway and masculine stride—and put her arms around my neck.

"You are completely out of your mind," she said and kissed me on the ear.

"I ain't nothin' but an assistant coach," I said.

"You are outrageous," she added.

"Yes, ma'am, I am."

"This is impossible."

"No, ma'am, it's supposed to work like a champ. I'm promised that it will run and you got a guarantee on the paint job that will last till the year 2000."

"You're crazy."

"Yes, ma'am."

"Crazy."

"Well, ma'am, they call us guys crazy like a fox."

"Oh," she said, with a wondrous leer. "You're trying to buy my affections?"

"Yes, ma'am, I have to confess. Now I'm just a country boy and, I'm wonderin' if the neighbors might get the wrong idea if you keep on bitin' my ear. We could go inside for a minute while we get our plans together. Hey, you're not supposed to cry!"

"Come with me, boy," she sniffled. "We've got a few things to do before we pack up for our vacation." She took me by the hand and led me upstairs.

If you are lucky, you might know what it is to associate yourself intimately with the Statue of Liberty—on the assumption of course that she wasn't looking so stern and wasn't made of copper or whatever. What I mean is, you have to imagine yourself of sufficient stature yourself to connect with a lady of mythic proportions, and suddenly there is a hurricane roaring through New York Harbor and you and Liberty are clutching each other, alive and swaying, and earthquakes start happening, great seismic rhythms, and the earth turns inside out and there's a wonderful fresh smell in your soul, like a forest cleansed by a rain, and you and the lady named Liberty are the only two people in the world who know about it. Maybe you can imagine it but I'd feel bad if you hadn't somewhere along the way experienced it.

Before long, Kendall Lea got up, stretching like a cheetah, and ambled off into the kitchen to fix a lunch, and within a half hour we were headed south on Route 25 for the two-hour drive to Truth or Consequences, eating ham sandwiches. Kendall Lea was behind the wheel, the top was down and, above the collar of her sheepskin jacket, her face was reddening with the chill.

"So how do you like it?" I asked.

"It's glorious!" she said with a vast sensuous grin. "It's gorgeous."

We watched the barren, brown landscape go by, a place of long reaches of hopeless land populated here and there by hopeless-looking ranches and less frequently by hopeless-looking little towns.

"Truth or Consequences," she said at one point. "That sounds sort of ominous. Why did they name it that?"

"You happen to be talking to an expert on that," I said. "Before your time there was a guy who had a radio show named that—a guy named Ralph Edwards. One of those early quiz show things. Anyway, this place used to be called Hot Springs because they have hot springs that people go to, and I guess business was bad or something, because the city voted around 1950 to take the name Truth or Consequences, like the radio show, in return for some annual festival or something. Thought it would bring in business, I guess. And maybe it did. They've got more motels in the place than people, but there isn't one motel you'd want to stay in. It's kind of a depressed area."

"So why does Dr. Deitweiler have a ranch here?"

I had to think who Dr. Deitweiler was since we never use that name for Taxbreak. "His accountant got him a good deal, I guess."

Taxbreak's ranch was east of the town about seven miles, in a place of brown rolling countryside and occasional rocky escarpments—a small place maybe 100 acres in all, most of which he didn't use. He didn't need most of them. What he needed was water and he had it, some other deal his accountant had made. Taxbreak got enough water from what was otherwise the Truth or Consequences supply to make a few handfuls of acres green—just the sort of thing female quarter horses like to graze in while awaiting their turn to be impregnated by Taxbreak's two megastuds. In return for the water, Taxbreak did all kinds of charitable things with his time to help the town fathers improve medical care in their dreary little part of the state.

As we bumped along the dirt track that led to Taxbreak's emerald isle, Kendall asked me if he was married.

"Oh, yeah. His wife's name is Lucia," I said. "Some people say Taxbreak married her before he knew he was going to be a bigshot doctor. She's Spanish. Not one of the old families that are class around here, but from a new family—maybe a generation or two here. So when Taxbreak began to hit the big time, everyone said he'd have to drop Lucia to get anywhere. But he loves her. I guess it's as simple as that. She doesn't say much around him."

"I get the feeling," said Kendall, "that most people don't say much around him."

"Center stage. A real showboat. Some people say he's tacky. But he's a helluva good orthopedist, the best, and you can put up with a lot for the best."

Kendall Lea looked ahead at the dips and turns in the dirt road. After a moment she said: "What's hard is learning to put up with the best."

I thought of a wisecrack, realized it wasn't time for a wisecrack, and we rounded a curve in the road and there before us was Taxbreak's ranch house, made of logs by one of those companies that put up new log houses for people who want to go rustic in Florida or northern California, except that Taxbreak's place was more like a log hotel. Below the house, down a lush green lawn, was a large series of matching log outbuildings. Barns, stables, the whole thing, all in matching logs, about as much a part of the natural landscape as an aluminum skyscraper in the Everglades. Somewhere in one of the little log outbuildings, his studs were humping away, a stream of equine semen flowing into the hopes and dreams of the only sportsmen immune from the tender loving care of the IRS.

"There's Lucia," I said, and waved. She was standing outside the Taxbreak Hotel wrapped in a shawl she had probably made herself. She stared, puzzled at the light lilac Cadillac approaching her from somewhere far outside her experience, waved limply, and then waved more enthusiastically as we pulled up nearby.

"Hey, where have you been?" she shouted as I stepped out of the car and hugged her.

"What d'you mean? You know where I've been. Portland, Seattle, Cleveland, you know. Last place."

"Nomads," she said cheerfully. "Good-for-nothing nomads. When are you going to settle down, young man?" She was short, by any standard, and very short by the standards of us freaks. She was hugging me around the waist, the greatest elevation she could reach in that manner of greeting.

"I'll settle down when I persuade Taxbreak to give me one of his quarter horses."

She disengaged, a large smile on her olive face. "And this is Kendall Lea who I read about? Yes, Kendall, I am so happy to meet you." She bustled around the bow of Kendall's Lea's lilac Cadillac and opened the door.

"Welcome. I am Lucia. Come with me. You must want to freshen up after that long drive." She paused. "What a car! It is yours?" Kendall Lea grinned.

"All mine," she said. "Isn't it beautiful?"

"Hey, Lucia," I asked. "Where's Taxbreak?"

She pointed to the complex of barns and outbuildings. "He's down there, overseeing the natural processes. Come with me, Kendall." And she bundled my big beautiful lady into the front door, jabbering all the while. I imagined that Lucia didn't have many women friends that she could easily see, given Taxbreak's meteoric career, and it didn't surprise me that she had needed but one look at Kendall Lea to see a friend. I ambled down the greensward to the barns.

A figure emerged in a light tan Stetson, old Levis, and a sheepskin jacket. I'd seen the jacket before: Lucia had embroidered it on the back with a slightly fanciful orange and purple quarter horse skeleton, like a medical textbook drawing. The figure waved.

"Hey! Looking good!" he shouted.

"What's looking good?" I asked, approaching him. He stuck out his hand, and I shook it.

"You guys. Christ, you've been playing better than .500 ball for a week and a half."

"Just basics," I said noncommitally.

"Yeah, basics," he replied, "but what did you do to Mo Flynn? I've had to work my ass off for your opponents the last week what with him so ugly now. And you guys don't pay me enough to take care of that kind of thing. By the way, you want to see something beautiful?"

He showed me into the constricted log corral where his most elegant quarter horse carries on with precision and vigor. Named Lucian—apparently after some famous ancient Greek doctor—the horse was jerking his head up and down, glistening brown and black, looking for all the world like a god, which of course, in a certain way of thinking, he was. Creator of a lineage. The trainer, a wizened old guy in blue jeans, was murmuring to the horse.

"It's all there, man," said Taxbreak. "Beauty. Power. All of it. So it was Mo Flynn who got hypnotized first, huh?" He climbed up on a fence and squatted on its upper log, boot heels (worth about $200 apiece) hooked into the next log down. I joined him.

"It's weird. She did talk to the kid a few times and somehow he seems to have gotten the message."

"That's not how it works." Taxbreak said. "The message doesn't come from outside. It's inside. People like Kendall Lea are locksmiths. Oh, get a load of this. Here comes Mariah. She's from California, Sacramento, and they figure she's going to have the world's most successful quarter horse foal. Look at old Lucian. Whoo! What stamina that sonofabitch has. Third one today. Makes me feel old."

A trainer with a black cowboy hat was gingerly walking the muscled mare into Lucian's turf when I turned and noticed Kendall Lea striding down the lawn towards us. Mariah was beautiful, lithe, strong, and darkly dangerous looking, her skin rippling over bunched muscle in some unimaginable nervousness, anticipation or maybe, for all I knew, resentment. Kendall Lea's arms swung with an abandon that could only be that of a thoroughbred.

"Hey, Svengali," Taxbreak called to her. "Want to watch the game of the century?" Kendall Lea swung up on the fence.

"Did you hear the story about the young guy, just home from the wars, who took over his old man's farm in Maine?" asked Taxbreak.

"Nope," said Kendall Lea.

"Well, he had this cow and one day he took it up the hill to the next farm where one of those old downeasterners had a bull."

There was a clatter like thunder in the enclosure where

hooves were flying and more than a ton of horse flesh was getting nervous. "Ssssst," said one of the trainers.

"Well, the old farmer wasn't there, but his daughter was," Taxbreak went on with a reptilian grin. "So the young farmer arranged with her to put his cow together with the bull. And so they were sitting on the fence of the corral, watching the cow and the bull, and the young farmer said to himself, jeez, I haven't done that for a while myself. And finally he says, 'Boy, I wish I was doing that.' And the farmer's daughter said, 'Well, go ahead, it's your cow.' "

And Taxbreak nearly died of laughter. Kendall Lea put her hand on mine and laughed good-naturedly. There were titanic surgings of muscle and drive in the log enclosure and I thought of a bumper sticker for Taxbreak's horse wagon: "People Have More Fun."

The sun was dropping behind the brown low hills behind us. "Let's go in and get a drink," the doctor said. "Go ahead, I'll meet you up there." He swung off the fence and went over to talk to his trainer while Kendall Lea and I strolled up the long green lawn to the big house.

"I grew up with a lawn," she said, "but this certainly seems bizarre."

"Wait till you see Phoenix," I replied, which was the first stop on our western swing. Time to think of that later. Inside the big log ranch house a gargantuan orange fire lit a dark-paneled room about half the size of a basketball court. It looked as if Taxbreak had bought out the entire American Western Art Association. The walls were covered with paintings of cowboys and Indians and horses and deserts, and there were at least a dozen sculptures in bronze of the same subjects.

"Look at that!" Kendall Lea said, pointing to a silvery, oval-shaped piece reflecting the flames from the hearth. It was about two feet high and sat on a pedestal of dark wood.

She went over to it. "Is it silver?"

"That would be a helluva lot of silver—too much for Taxbreak even." I felt the metal. "Probably stainless steel." It was a pair of otters, one diving after another as if they were playing in the water. "Yup," I said. "See, ma'am, it says here on this here plate: *Ring of Bright Water,* stainless steel, Kent Ulberg."

Taxbreak came in the room.

"Do you like that one? It's one of my favorites. I got it in a silent auction at the Cowboy Hall of Fame. Sit down. Lucia's making some margaritas." We settled into the large, deep sofas that flanked the fireplace, and as we did so, Lucia arrived carrying a tray of bell-shaped glasses rimmed with salt. She passed them out and sat next to Kendall Lea.

"Kendall, don't you find it a little strange?" she asked with a smile.

"Strange?"

"Yes, being the first woman ever to be on the staff of a National Basketball Association team?"

"I'd never really thought of it that way," said Kendall, her face turned thoughtful.

"Hey," said Taxbreak. "You're the Sally Ride of the NBA." She grinned. "And," Taxbreak went on, "you're also the booster rocket. As the Albuquerque Demons begin the slow takeoff from the launchpad, gaining speed and hurtling into orbit, they will get their thrust, their power, from our secret weapon: hypnosis. Let's drink a toast."

"That's very nice," said Kendall Lea with a little smile on her face, "but I think it's a little exaggerated. Wouldn't basketball's Sally Ride be the first woman player? And, I don't think hypnosis is . . ."

"Oh, I wasn't talking about toasting that," said Taxbreak, standing. "Here's to your twenty-sixth birthday. Cheers."

He gulped down the margarita, and Kendall Lea blushed.

"Thank you." She looked at me and her blue eyes glowed. There was a little crinkle around them.

"Look," said Taxbreak. "I've got a birthday present for you. I forgot to wrap it." He started out of the room, paused, making a couple of swift gestures like hand signals to his wife and vanished, returning a moment later with a brown felt bag in his hand. It was about eight inches tall.

"Here, open it," said Taxbreak, a grin stretching virtually from ear to ear.

Kendall Lea's long fingers tugged at the string. "It's heavy," she said appreciatively. The mouth of the bag open, she reached in and shrieked.

"Oh my god!" she said. "This is . . . this is . . ."

"Take it out, will you?" I said. "I'm dying of suspense." Lucia was giggling. Kendall Lea withdrew the object from the bag. It was a small replica of the otters, in stainless steel.

"I liked 'em so much I commissioned the guy to do a bunch of small ones for special occasions."

Kendall looked at me. "Can I kiss the team doctor?"

"*I* wouldn't," I said, "but there's no team regulation about it. I don't think it ever came up before."

Kendall Lea stood up and embraced Taxbreak who said, "Shucks." She sat down next to Lucia and embraced her.

"I can't believe it. I love it. I'm so . . ." and she burst into tears the second time that day. Lucia patted her shoulder in the manner that is no doubt common to human history for several thousand years.

"It's so lovely," Kendall Lea said after she had stopped crying. "I love it." She looked up. "What a day! What a birthday! I love birthdays."

"It is hard to be away from your own family on important occasions like that," said Lucia. "We have thought a lot about how lonely it must be for you here . . ."

"Oh, no, Lucia, not lonely, it's so exciting, so different."

"Yes, but still, we wanted you to feel like part of the family."

Taxbreak interrupted. "See, we know what you're doing but we figured it must be . . . well, weird, with all these big jocks and in a strange part of the world and no real home and all that—traveling with this team is something I don't have to do, but I imagine it's an enormous pain in the ass and so the brilliant young assistant coach and I thought since your birthday coincided with a schedule break . . ."

"As opposed to a tax break," I said.

"Knock it off," Taxbreak said and turned back to Kendall Lea. "I'm trying to tell you that some of us are very, very happy you're here and we want you to know that you're welcome. As a matter of fact, we're very much aware that you're going to have an enormous effect on this team. Already have, as far as I can tell." He raised his voice. "Right, Mo?"

And from the kitchen three giants towered into the room, holding margaritas. "Surprise," they said shyly.

"No crying," I whispered. "Three's bad luck."

"You sweet man," she said.

Mo Flynn, Del Babbit, and Raphael Flint all came up and shook hands with Kendall Lea and said, "Happy Birthday." It was like pupils in school coming to the teacher except it was bizarre, upside down, what with the pupils towering over the teach. Kendall Lea beamed with such warmth that the guys soon got over their shyness.

"Is Dora here?" asked Kendall.

"Oh yeah," said Raphael with the semidemi glare that those who know him take as a smile. "She's out in the kitchen cookin' soul food. Us black folks may be outnumbered here but we gonna dominate the game."

It was nearly one o'clock when everyone shuffled off to the many bedrooms in Taxbreak Hotel with stomach cramps from the general hilarity. It was a peculiar quirk of Taxbreak's that he did not have heat in his ranch house—at least, not a furnace or anything like that. Each bedroom had a wood stove and a small pile of logs. Kendall Lea and I didn't bother lighting a fire though sleeping with a fire is one of God's luxuries. I didn't need anything as trivial as that.

Kendall Lea sat on the bed. It was covered with a white cottony quilt a foot thick. Taxbreak had told me that he'd bought twelve of them in Switzerland.

"I'm overcome," she said. I didn't say anything. She turned to me and her eyes watered over a bit.

"No, no," I said. "Two is all you get in a day."

"I love you," she said and crawled under the covers with their balloon of a quilt. And standing in my shorts at the foot of the bed, I drove on a guard, swiveled around him, dribbled past a ten-foot forward and leapt, hanging under the basket, floating in midair for twenty-five (count 'em) seconds and laid the ball up and it kissed the glass and ticked the rim and fell through the threads and we won the game and I leapt into bed under Taxbreak's Swiss quilt and flew with my lady like an eagle, free and proud and fine, the two of us, soaring over continents and oceans, in orbit.

9 "SHE'S A HYPNOTIST, right?" Dumfrey Schwartz was lolling in the chair across from my desk. "Right?"

"Dumfrey," I said, "it's none of your business what she is. She's a member of the training staff and we call her a human factors analyst."

"And she puts the guys in a trance before the game so they go out and play .500 ball, right?"

"Wrong, Dumfrey."

"What does she use, a crystal on a string? *Sleep,* Raphael, sleep. You're going to go out there and get offensive rebounds. That kind of stuff, right? Pendulums."

"Dumfrey, you are a huge pain in the ass, amazingly huge for someone your size."

The little man waggled his fingers at me voodoo-style and said, "Sleep, sleep."

"You've got it almost entirely wrong, Dumfrey, and I'm going to ask you something." The reporter sat up in his chair expectantly. "I'm going to tell you a bit about what Kendall Lea does around here and I'm going to ask you to print only as much of it as I tell you to. Get it?"

Dumfrey grinned and leaned forward.

"Are you talking about muzzling the press?"

"Listen, asshole, I can throw you out of here right now and you can spend the rest of the season wimping around trying to figure out what our training staff does and you'll never get it right. Now, I'm going to tell you and I'm going to tell you what you can say about it and if you ever let anyone know the rest, I am personally going to knock you through your skinny little knees. Do you understand, Dumfrey?"

"Sure, Coach. I understand." He sat back in his chair looking conspiratorial. I explained in some detail about neurolinguistics, about finding moments in someone's life when they were excellent.

"They call those times demon states," I said, "Nice, huh?"

"Demon states," Dumfrey repeated. "Demon states."

"You got it, Dumfrey, good boy. And that is all you can say about it in the paper or anywhere else. You can say that Kendall Lea is a specialist in Human Factors and Group Dynamics. You can make her sound like a sociologist. And you can say that the guys are in a demon state when they win."

"I love it," said Dumfrey, licking his lips.

"Any more than that, Dumfrey, you little frog, and I'll dismember you with an icepick."

"I love it," said Dumfrey. "You have my word." He stood up, raised a pallid clenched fist in a gesture of what I suppose was solidarity, and scuttled out of the office.

That afternoon we flew to Phoenix and took on the Suns. Phoenix is no great ball club but they had beaten us twice already this season. They're fast and they play the transition game—fast breaks and all that—better than most teams in our conference, but they're thin on defense. Our strategy was to slow them down, keep them from running, play a deliberate game of set plays. To do this means you've got to have defense yourself, muscle. It's not a pretty way to play but it can be effective. And it was that night.

Mo Flynn took them by surprise. Teams still hadn't really picked up on the change in Mo. He came in toward the end of the first quarter, when we were behind 23 to 18 and took over. On his first defensive play, he went up on the Suns' center and nearly rammed the ball down his throat. Down court, at our end, he took a pass, shoveled it off to Fast Fred and set a pick that sent the Suns' center reeling out of bounds while Fred sailed off toward the basket.

It can happen like that and often does. A guy comes in off the bench and does something dramatic right off the bat and the whole tempo changes. The team got hot and by half time we were ahead by eleven points. The second half was mostly elbows and grunts, warfare. The Suns' shooting guard got thrown out of the game for taking a swipe at Raphael Flint after a particularly brutal battle for a rebound. I don't know what Raphael did to the guy in there in the crowd but he jumped at Raphael and hit him on the arm to the accompaniment of the refs' whistles and out he went, with Raphael just standing there, hands on his hips, glaring with contempt. Then he shook his head and took off down court to shoot his foul shot.

We beat the Suns by 17 points, the biggest margin all season and Jim Munson strode off the court with the suggestion of a smile on his face. The next morning I got a copy of the Albuquerque *Journal* from the hotel lobby and went back upstairs. Kendall Lea was curled up under the covers, her blond hair spread out like liquid gold over the pillow.

"Get a load of this," I said.

"What's that?" she asked sleepily.

"Dumfrey."

"Oh god, what's he said now?"

"Listen." I sat down on the bed and Kendall Lea hitched her knees up, touching me through the covers.

"Something extraordinary happened last night in Phoenix. Something so extraordinary that we need a new term for it. The Demons, sparked by sixth man Mo Flynn, took off like a rocket. It was as if Zeus decided to send a thunderbolt down in the last few minutes of the first quarter. Mo Flynn was that thunderbolt, titanic picks that had the Suns reeling, shots blocked with devastating authority. In minutes the Demons converted the electricity into sheer power. The Suns were eclipsed. The Demons were inspired—no, it's as if they were under some supernatural influence. Call it a Demon State."

I put the paper down. "He does run on, doesn't he?" I said.

"You told him," said Kendall Lea, with a little smile, the one that suggests the existence of a cosmic joke.

"Yep. I told him the whole thing, and I told him that if he spilled the beans, he would be fried in little strips. He loved the idea of demon states."

"I bet the fans love it too."

"You got it, beautiful." I stood up. "Wait till we get back to Albuquerque. Why don't you haul your big, beautiful lazy body out of there and we'll get some breakfast." Kendall Lea gets out of bed slowly and goes through a series of ritual stretches, something like Japanese theater, and I watched her even though it probably wasn't polite. She didn't mind, as far as I could tell, and she smiled at me, shook her hair around and strode off to the bathroom. "You," she said, "are slick, my friend. Slick."

"Just a country boy," I said, as the sound of the shower masked her giggle.

Played properly and by the best talent—like Philadelphia in 1982—basketball is in my opinion the highest form of art, an original invented-in-America art form. We imported painting and sculpture and ballet and all that from Europe and we never invented anything in the arts ourselves—unless you think that nitwit who covers peninsulas in plastic wrap is an artist. We've just copied the Old Country. But we invented professional sports and they are now the pageantry and most accessible art in America. Baseball is a mathematical art, a game of angles, like when painters learned about perspective. Slow. Majestic. Classic. A kind of quiet that builds on itself, punctuated always with surprises. Football is the martial arts. If you think football is thinly disguised thuggery, you never noticed the tactics and strategy, the elegant craftsmanship that is going on in every contact between each pair of monsters on the field. There's a lot of mind in football. It scares me a bit since it is also a legal way of getting killed, but watching an offense go eighty yards to score when there's only one minute left in the game is an aesthetic experience that leaves you gasping in awe— even reverence.

But of course basketball is my idea of the highest art. It has pattern, rhythm, grace, symmetry and assymetry and, like other sports, moral truth: someone wins. There are rules and forms and within those there is improvisation. No choreographer could produce anything like it. What ballet troupe could do its thing if, in the process, it also had to put a round ball through a hoop fifty times during the performance? Of if they didn't know how the dance was supposed to end?

Kendall Lea told me, when I broached this theory to her, that it was interesting but would probably not make much of a dent among the curators of the Metropolitan Museum of Art. Still, I think of basketball as the highest form of art and also a properly American art because it's democratic. Anyone can put up a hoop in an alley and play. Anyone who has a TV can watch the giant gazelles of the NBA do their dance eighty-one times a year.

Not that the Albuquerque Demons were playing basket-ball like an art form. Except for an occasional soaring swoop by Fast Fred, we were playing basketball like Cro-Magnon men attacking a mastodon. Picks. Elbows. Muscle. A kind of thuggery. Lots of fouls. It was all we could do. And we won three out of four games on that road trip—Phoenix, San Diego, and Golden State. Los Angeles ran past us like we were out for a pizza, but they do that to everyone. Kendall Lea had two more sessions with Raphael during the road trip and an initial session with Del Babbitt, the center. Raphael was amazing people by this time, not by getting his old jumper back (which he had) and not by occasionally changing gears and charging the hoop for dunks and once—in San Diego—a hook shot that he hadn't used for eight years, but by passing the ball.

It was in the third quarter against Golden State and Isaiah had gotten the ball to Raphael who started jigging his ass around and everyone knew he was going to fake and dip and turn around for his shot. A guard sagged on him so it was two on one, and the center moved toward the basket and Raphael jigged and I swear to God, without looking, hurled the ball behind him across the court to Fast Fred who was wide open in the corner. Two points.

"Did you see *that?*" I shouted at Kendall Lea who was sitting a few perches down the bench with the trainer.

She shook her head, smiling. The buzzer sounded the end of the quarter and the guys ambled off the court, look-ing cool. The team huddled around Big Jim and his clip-board for another refresher course in strategy and, before joining them, I went over to Kendall Lea.

"Don't you watch the damn games?" I asked.

"Usually."

"That was a great play. Raphael simply didn't do that before you started working on him. What the hell were you looking at?"

"You."

"Me?"

"Your face." She smiled. "I can tell what's happening by watching your face."

I went over to the huddle and didn't hear anything. Goddamn hypnotist.

On the way back from California, on the plane, the guys were all cramped into those seats that are too little for normal people, most of them listening to music through their Walkman earphones. Mo Flynn was reading a science fiction novel. The other passengers in the plane had gotten over gawking and the autograph hounds had been satisfied. I was sleepy; it was a late flight after the game. Kendall Lea was sitting beside me, her head back against the seatback, looking off into space.

"You awake?" she asked.

"Yep."

"Del Babbitt shouldn't be playing center."

I looked over at her.

"What do you mean?"

She put her hand to her throat and fingered a turquoise eagle she had bought in Phoenix. The wings were on little hinges and it hung around her neck on a delicate silver chain.

"When he was a kid, he loved music."

"Kendall . . ."

"Especially ballet music. He tried out for the local performance of *The Nutcracker* and got a part. He was about ten. The next year he tried out again but he had grown four and a half inches. He was too big."

"So why shouldn't he play center? He's seven feet tall, for chrissakes."

"Playing center doesn't match his demon state. He had a little solo in *The Nutcracker,* sort of floating around the action. It's riveted in his unconscious mind."

"Jesus H. Christ," I said. "And we thought Fast Fred was our ballerina."

"Play Del at forward," said Kendall Lea. "He'll do better there."

"Who'd play center?"

"That's your problem, my man. All I can do is analyze human factors." She smiled and closed her eyes and I had a sense that the cosmic joke was on track, unstoppable, heading inevitably for some off-the-wall punch line.

The next night, after the plane ride back from California and eight hours of sleep at the wrong time of day, we confronted the Washington Bullets. The NBA schedule is probably the most inhumane affair devised since they invented airplanes that can make computers think that humans function after being whisked back and forth across a continent day after day. You'd think that the jerks who make schedules . . . well, that's a problem for someone else. My job was just to back up Big Jim, and keep an eye on things like Raphael Flint's slight limp, an unnoticeable (to most, I hoped) response to failing knees, and to ponder the arcane readings of tea leaves perpetrated upon the guys by the most beautiful lady who ever lived or ever will.

Have I told you lately how much I loved her? Sure, there was business to transact, she popping little surprises on me about once a day like Dell Babbitt tripping the light fantastic in a pair of tights at ten years old, and to be sure, there was a lot that she was withholding from me—some grand strategy forming in her magnificent, sweet mind—but my first reaction to her, formed in a daze in Moriarity's Irish Pub in Portland, had never given up any of its original luster. Every time I looked at Kendall Lea or thought about her I was overwhelmed with a sense of calm and, somewhere back of my diaphragm, a burst of glowing fireworks. Nobody's perfect, they say, and Kendall had a few habits that didn't jibe with my little notions of things. For example, she loaded up my apartment with so many house plants that sometimes I tripped over the damn things. She had no respect for doorways—each one was clogged with a house plant. And when she watered the goddamned things, she poured water over them with abandon, making big stains on the floor.

Did I complain?

Let me ask you something. If an angel came into your house, and passed over you a wand in such a way that there was an unquenchable light, a continuous warmth like the glow of a hearth that you used to enjoy aimlessly and without thought for hours on end as a little kid, mindlessly watching the patterns of the fire, knowing that you were completely okay, would you complain?

Kendall Lea made love to me with her eyes. A slight turn of her head, the most minor gesture of her long fingers, even the way she stood, like some out-of-this-world stork, gracefully bending over a sickly asparagus fern, clucking and cooing, or stretching her wondrous lithe body after a good night's sleep, all of this simply told me that I was the single most fortunate graduate of Rifle, Colorado, High School, the greatest achiever ever to set foot at the University of Colorado, the unquestioned winner in the game of life, a genius. Life without Kendall Lea was unimaginable. Once you've been dusted with starlight, you don't settle for anything less, and the world is good.

Anyway, the Washington Bullets were like us, the Demons. A bit low on the talent scale but high on muscle. It was brute strength against brute strength and in such situations, tempers run high. Nobody gets mad at the goddamn Lakers because they fly around doing basketball as it should be done. You can't get mad at that, even though you can get humiliated. But the Bullets play their games in the trenches, like us. It was an ugly game and the refs must have been imported from Congress because every call went against us. Raphael had four fouls by half-time, giving him two more before he fouled out, and Mo Flynn had three. Jim Munson was in the midst of a slow burn by the middle of the third quarter, when we were behind by eight points and Raphael had picked up his fifth foul. Before Big Jim could get the stupid ref to realize he was calling for a time-out, Raphael got caught in a crowd, going for the ball, and the whistle sounded and the ref called a foul. On Raphael. Now it was obvious to all 15,000 people in the arena that Raphael was the one who'd been victimized (that time) but the ref pointed at Raphael.

Big Jim, who had already screamed at the refs a few times and was getting red, stood up from the bench and took one step forward, his arm raised like he was carrying a club.

And then the world stopped.

The crowd was booing, a sound that rose and redoubled and echoed, a huge tide of outrage, filling the arena. Two of our players were on their feet off the bench, looks of unbelief on their faces. Raphael was glaring with such intensity I thought the ref might turn into vapor on the spot. Isaiah mouthed the word "sheee-it" with sufficient clarity to make it clear to every TV viewer what he thought of the call. And Big Jim Munson, red-faced, arm-raised, hand clenched, suddenly looked perplexed, like a kid who had seen something he doesn't understand, and keeled over backwards, knocking the bench over. He fell backwards like a board, hand raised, and hit the floor. Fifteen thousand booing fans went dead silent, and Jim Munson's face, still with its bewildered look, went white, like the changing of a traffic light.

Before I could move, a form flashed past me. Taxbreak. He had a seat behind the bench and came to most·of the home games. He could have sat on the bench with the rest of us but he said he should be a paying customer since we needed the money and he didn't. Anyway, Taxbreak flew past and crouched over the Coach, pounding on his chest and breathing huge bursts of air into his mouth. Taxbreak was engaged in this frantic activity and Big Jim was as still as a rock and it looked like something from another world, a different kind of play, as if a theater had gone mad. Within minutes, guys with a stretcher arrived and carefully lifted Big Jim aboard and left. The arena was in chaos.

What the fuck does a basketball arena do when a guy on center stage seems to have died. I ran after the stretcher and caught up with Taxbreak.

"Is he dead?" I asked.

"No. But it's bad. Bad. A big motherfucker of an attack."

"Well, shit . . ."

"I'll take care of it," said Taxbreak, and I remembered he had been in Vietnam and felt better. "Go on," he said. "Finish." And he ran down the dimly lit corridor after the stretcher. There were lights shining in the arena, the usual lights but they were blinding when I got back to the bench. They were reporters swarming over the floor and the crowd was silent. I went over to the officials and told them that it was a heart attack.

"What the hell do we do now?" asked one of the refs.

"How the hell do I know?" I said.

Tub Bligh approached the group of officials. Tub not only owned the Demons but the Arena. "What happened? Heart attack?"

"Yes sir. Taxbreak is with him in the ambulance."

"Holy shit," said Tub Bligh. "What do we do now?"

"I don't know," I said. The players were standing near the bench, the Bullets doing the same on the other side of the court.

"Holy shit," said Tub Bligh.

"Maybe you better get off to the hospital," I suggested. "Maybe we should cancel the game. I mean . . ."

"This has never happened," said the Demons' owner. "What the hell do you do?"

"Taxbreak said to finish," I said.

Then Tub Bligh did something that most people might not have thought to do and perhaps that is why he is an owner, not an employee. He went over to Raphael Flint and took him by the elbow and said something. Raphael glowered and nodded his head. Then Tub went over to the row of tables where the record keepers and the microphones are located. He picked up a microphone in his big fist and began to talk to the buzzing crowd.

"Ladies and gentlemen." The voice boomed through the amplifier and the crowd fell silent. "We have had a very tragic occurrence here. Coach Munson has had a heart attack. I want to assure you that he is under the best medical care, our team doctor, Dr. Deitweiler, is with him and he is on the way to the hospital where I am sure he will receive the finest medical care. This is an awful thing . . . an awful thing . . . and I am sure that you all join me in wishing Coach Munson the blessings of God and a quick recovery.

"I have every confidence that Coach Munson *will* recover. He is a competitor. A fiercely competitive man who loves life and honors excellence. A man who cares for his players as if they were his family. I am confident that, if he were able to do so, he would request that this game resume, because Coach Munson has always been interested not only in the way a game is played but in its outcome. He likes winning.

"Therefore, while this tragic moment must afflict us all in many ways, and not knowing exactly how Coach Munson is doing is an unbearable pall, I think we should carry on, as he would wish.

"I would like to ask that we all bow our heads and pray for Big Jim Munson and to wish that at this terrible crisis in his life he will—with the grace of the Lord—achieve his most important demon state."

And Tub Bligh bowed his head, standing there with a microphone in his big fist, and we could hear him breathe over the loudspeaker, and the 15,000 fans were silent as death. The teams had somehow managed to line up in front of their benches, the way they do for the national anthem before the game, and their heads were bowed.

"All right," said Tub Bligh, after a few moments. "All right. We pray for a great man and we will honor him by doing what he loves best. We will play basketball. The Washington Bullets honor us here in Albuquerque with their presence and their competitive spirit. Gentlemen?" And Tub Bligh bowed to the refs.

The game resumed, the weirdest few minutes I think I've ever experienced, with guys floating around doing their various things as if in a dream. When the buzzer sounded, ending the third quarter, I realized that for three and a half minutes of playing time there had not been a sound from the crowd. Eerie. During the break, the players returned to the bench and sat down. I made no move to gather them for any conversation. There were 15,000 stunned people in there. Tub Bligh came up to the bench and took me by the elbow.

"You're acting coach," he said. "Big Jim will be okay but he's out for . . . well, he's out indefinitely. A massive cardiac arrest and thank god for Taxbreak or he'd be dead. Anyway, Jim's going to survive. I'll tell them."

He went over to the desk where the microphones were and stepped over the tangle of wires, grasping the announcer's mike.

"Ladies and gentlemen. I have heard from Dr. Deitweiler, the team doctor, that Coach Munson is resting comfortably and that the crisis is past. The coach will be fine."

There was applause and a few whistles.

"I understand that Coach Munson has in fact asked about this game. He wants you all to know that he is most desirous that the game be played and that the Demons, with all due respect to our friends from Washington, beat the pants off them." Tub Bligh grinned, a huge toothy smear in a great red piece of meat. The crowd roared its approval and the refs blew their whistles and the fourth quarter began.

There arose, at that moment, just as the ref handed the ball to Isaiah Jones to bring in bounds, a sound the likes of which I had never heard, a long and maniacal-sounding shriek like a hurricane wind, echoing around the arena: 15,000 people from the Albuquerque metropolitan region were praying in a way that no one had ever heard before.

DEEEEEEEEEEEEEEEE-Mon-STAAAAAAAAAAATE!

Over and over again.

DEEEEEEEEEEEEEEEE-Mon-STAAAAAAAAAAAAATE!

The place reverberated with it. It got to be like a round,

where the fans were shouting just behind their own echo. The arena filled with sound.

DEEEEEEEEEEEEEEEEE-Mon-STAAAAAAAAAATE
DEEEEEEEEEEEEEEEEE-Mon-STAAAAAAAAAATE
DEEEEEEEEEEEEEEEEE-Mon-STAAAAAAAAAATE

As I recall, we won by three points. It didn't matter. After the game we all went to the hospital and sat around even though there was no way we could see the coach and nothing to do except listen to the doctor when he would come out and say that everything was as good as could be expected, Big Jim would survive, and why didn't we go home, nice game by the way, and all that, but we just all sat there till the sun came up, not saying much. Big Jim's wife was in the room with him, of course, and took the call from the Commissioner, and Tub Bligh came in around six o'clock in the morning with a bunch of bacon sandwiches and after we ate, still no one talking much, I said, "Well, we got Seattle tonight. Better get some rest." So the guys filed out of the hospital, gawked at by the people in the emergency waiting room, and I drove home, a silent Kendall Lea sitting next to me in the Checker.

I pulled into the parking space in front of my building and turned off the ignition.

"Jeez. What do we do now?" I said, more a statement than a question.

Kendall Lea put her hand on my knee. "Lead," she said. "You're a born leader."

10 ALL THE TEAMS have at least a couple of them—a starter and a substitute. They're point guards or play makers. They're usually smaller than the rest of the team, rarely more than six-four. They're the sure-handed guys, quick and fast, who get the ball downcourt and signal plays like Winston Churchill making the victory sign, and do stutter steps, dribble behind their backs, and get assists, which is when you pass the ball off to a guy who scores. These are the guys who control the pace of a game, the ones who get things started. A good one can do all of the above and also drive to the basket between the monsters for a lay-up, a good way to keep the big guys on the opposing team honest—meaning that they have to worry about more than one man. Good point guards own the ball, and let the other guys play with it.

Their job is to handle the ball, in short. You don't want big guys handling the ball too much. A center who dribbles the ball is usually not long for the NBA. Centers get passes and pass off or shoot. When they get a rebound they get rid of the ball fast. Most forwards are also too big to handle the ball much. Shoot. Rebound. Maybe a couple of dribbles by way of creating confusion, but as a standard practice, you don't want the big guys to put the ball on the floor. Theirs is an aerial game.

The point guard is the one who lives on the floor. Our

point guard was on cocaine. He was backed up by a rookie kid who simply didn't know the ropes yet.

"So how's the program going, Isaiah?" I asked. He was sitting in the chair across from my desk in my eight-by-eight cubicle. He looked down at his foot which rested on his knee, lanky legs making a precise geometry.

"It's okay, man."

"Okay?" I asked.

"Yeah. Okay. I talk to the doctor, he talks to me."

"And?"

"I'm gettin off it." He looked up at me and back at his foot. He was twenty-seven years old. He had been born in Patrick County, Virginia, a backwater county where white people still called his family coloreds. He had grown up in the northern part of the county, tobacco land, and had gained a certain prominence in high school as an athlete and a wise-ass. Basketball had become his ticket out of the shreds of the Civil War that still lay tattered in the minds of Patrick County and he had gone to the more cosmopolitan life of North Carolina State where he became not just a star but a big shot, and was drafted on the second round by the pros. Another *nouveau riche* yokel at play in the arenas of Big Time. He divorced his college-sweetheart wife after two years in the NBA and lived it up, a genius in the backcourt, a great one-on-one player, a hero to his people back home but, before long, an addict—not just to coke but to a flimsy view of himself as a big shot. I didn't like him very much.

"We need you full-time," I said. "You missed practice today."

Isaiah's eyes hooded over. "Look, man, I play hard. So I'm late for a practice. So what?" he smiled ingratiatingly. "I got twelve assists against the Bullets, didn't I? And fourteen points?"

"But," I said, "the game before that you were somewhere else, right? Your mind was not present."

"I'm . . ." Isaiah said, and looked off into space.

"Isaiah. Isaiah. I've been fair to you, haven't I? I've kept all this cocaine shit from Tub Bligh. But now I'm responsible for everything around here until they get a new coach. I need 100 percent of Isaiah Jones. He's one of the best."

Isaiah looked up at me and looked away, studying his shoes.

"So I'm going to have to ask you to do something," I said.

"Look, man, I don't want to talk to no hypnotist. I got a problem with coke and I'm taking care of it . . . my way." Isaiah stood up. "I don't believe in women in basketball. Maybe you think she's got the answer to *your* problem but she ain't got the . . . she don't . . ." Isaiah jigged around in frustration. "Women don't belong here. I ain't talkin to a woman."

"Listen, Isaiah," I said. "You've got one hope. Just one. One hope in life. You are good at handling a basketball and if you blow that, you're dead. A street bum. And you're about to blow it, I'm telling you. You're not good enough to miss practices. You're just not that good. No one is. Now sit down."

He jerked his head sideways and looked off into the distance, then sat down.

"I ain't talking to no woman," he said.

"You don't have to talk to her."

"Good."

"But you've got to beat her at your game."

Isaiah looked up bewildered. "What the hell does that mean?"

"Would you arm-wrestle for me for $500?" I asked. Isaiah nodded. "Why?" I asked.

"Because I could probably win."

"Maybe. We'll try it sometime. Meanwhile do you think you could beat a lady hypnotist?"

"At *arm*-wrestling?"

"At your game."

Isaiah stood up again. "This isn't a basketball team. It's ... it's ... I don't know what the fuck it is." He turned, back as straight as a board.

"I've got $500 here that says you can't beat her, Isaiah."

"Sheeeee ..." he said and walked out the door. I punched out the numbers of Kendall Lea's extension.

"Hello," she said.

"I just talked to Isaiah. He's furious."

"Good."

"I told him he'd have to reckon with you. I told him we needed him whole."

"Wonderful."

"You think it will work? I mean ..."

"Hey, Coach, would I let you down?" She hung up the phone and I looked at my end of it for a while. This is crazy.

I had an appointment with Tub Bligh at his office downtown so I got up and went to the door. I could hear the high voice of Raphael Flint.

"Look, kid," Raphael was saying. "These are tough times. Coach Munson gone and all that. But we beginnin to play, now, *play*. I don't want you to screw it up, hear? You do what the coach says, boy."

"Don't you be wuffin at me," said Isaiah Jones. "I don't like threats."

"No threat, man," said Raphael. "No threat. Just advice."

I walked out into the hall. Raphael looked over at me. "Hey, Coach," he said. "Hear anything more about Big Jim?"

"I called the hospital an hour ago. They say he's resting comfortably."

"That's what they always say. How can a man be resting comfortably after an attack like that?" Raphael glared with contempt for the medical profession, and I took off down the hall for my meeting with the owner.

Tub Bligh's offices are on the third floor of a downtown building and it always strikes me as silly to see "Sandia Molybdenum Company" painted on the big glass wall, followed by "Albuquerque Demons." But both outfits are run from the one set of offices, no matter how incongruous it seems. The receptionist smiled and nodded and pushed some buttons on her phone. I sat down and glanced through *Sports Illustrated*, seeing nothing about us in that issue. The only other stuff to read was metallurgical journals. In a few minutes, Tub Bligh's secretary, Julia, came into the reception room. A tall, thin woman in her forties, she wore dark-rimmed spectacles, a dark suit, and dark shoes. She smiled. "Hi," I said.

"Come along with me," she said pleasantly. "This is an awful thing, isn't it? Such a terrible shock." I made the appropriate noises as we walked down a long, office-lined corridor to the walnut doors where Tub Bligh did his captain-of-industry number. Julia opened the door for me and I went in.

Tub Bligh was facing the window behind his desk, the phone clenched in his hand.

"$3.02?" he said. "That's ridiculous."

He was silent.

"But $3.02 is the worst price since 1982, January."

Pause.

"Well, shit, okay. Get rid of the stuff."

He turned to face me, dropping the phone into its cradle from about six inches up. Tub Bligh is a jowly version of Willard Scott, the national weatherman, a large, forceful man with big hips and thighs which he doesn't try to disguise by fancy tailoring but displays happily, as if, over a lot of years of good eating, he had earned them.

"Jeez," he said. "They're ruining me. These goddam oil companies, opening up molybdenum mines when we're already in a glut. I mean, I've got a hundred thousand tons of the stuff on the *ground* and I've got to keep mining so I don't lose customers. They want molybdenum, I give them molybdenum. Well, that's not your problem. I'm losing money faster on molybdenum than basketball. This too will pass, as my mother used to say. Look, I've got high hopes for this ball club."

"So do I, Mr. Bligh."

"It costs me thousands of dollars a day to field the Demons every night. I love the Demons. I have high hopes for them this year. You've been playing well lately."

Tub Bligh leaned back in his high-backed leather chair. He smiled. Then he frowned.

"A bad business, this."

I waited silently, not knowing whether he was speaking of basketball or molybdenum.

"Jim's heart attack," he said. "A shocking tragedy."

"Just awful," I said.

"How's morale?" asked Tub.

"Hard to say, sir, everyone is still in shock."

"Yeah, of course. Well, courage, my father used to tell me, is keeping going, doing all the necessary things, in spite of any setback." He leaned forward, put his elbows on his desk and intertwined his fingers in a cathedral arch of flesh. He hadn't uttered his father's homily with any kind of portentousness—it was more as if he were simply reminding himself. I didn't know this man well at all. Over the two years I'd been with the Demons, I'd met with him maybe fifteen times, usually in the locker room after a win at home. I decided I liked him.

"Well," he went on, "you're in charge now, boy, for the rest of the season. You're Acting Coach and I mean that with a capital A and a capital C. We'll have a press conference at 4:00 P.M. to announce that. You understand that I can't make you Coach now, what with the nature of the season . . ." He paused. I nodded. "But you're in charge. You run the team."

"Thank you, sir. I'll do my best."

Tub Bligh stared over my head. It didn't seem to be a dismissal, so I sat still and looked at the photographs arrayed on the wall behind him—group shots of grinning freaks towering over a happy Tub in the locker room and ragged, torn bits of landscape cut to pieces by Sandia mining equipment, basketball and mining all mixed up together. I wondered how—and if—this man could separate the two in his mind.

"You going to make any changes?" he asked me.

"We're playing pretty well, like you said. I hope we don't have to."

Tub Bligh leaned back. "You're in charge. You run the team. But that fella, Packer, he isn't performing.

"He's steady, sir, and we need that."

"And Spokes, he doesn't rebound. We need rebounds. Do you think that shrink is going to get him on the boards?" Tub smiled conspiratorialy.

"She's working on it," I said. "Actually, she isn't a . . ."

"Oh, I know, boy. I know what she is. A hypnotist. Christ, maybe when she's through with the team she could work on my sales division." His face lit up. "Hey, why not? Does she have any spare time these days?"

"She's pretty busy with the guys," I said.

"Just kidding, son." Tub Bligh smiled again. "Maybe after the season. How do you think we'll finish this season?" He looked me in the eye. Courage, his father had said, was to carry on regardless of setbacks.

"In the play-offs," I said. Tub Bligh stood up and I followed suit. He led me to the door with a beefy hand on my shoulder.

"You do that," he said as he opened the door, "and it will save me the trouble of hunting around for a head coach for the next few seasons."

I walked down the corridor to the reception room, thinking about carrots and sticks.

"Congratulations," said the receptionist with a smile and I nodded thanks and let myself out through the glass doors. It was eleven o'clock. I had time to go over to the hospital before afternoon practice. It was a cold, crisp Albuquerque day and I wound the driver's side window down on the Checker as I headed for the freeway that led to the other side of town, in a sense feeling the need for a cold shower of some sort. In the play-offs, I had said. In the play-offs. Jerk. Pin your future on a dream. What kind of damn fool pins his future on a dream?

Big Jim Munson looked terrible—shrunken, white, even gray. He was in intensive care, festooned with tubes and chromium contraptions, bathed in a low, overhead light that nevertheless seemed to glare. The nurse, a quiet and expressionless Chicano woman, had said that I could have a couple of minutes with him. His eyes slowly moved in my direction as I went in, trying not to make too much noise with my boots on the linoleum floor.

"Hi, Coach," I said.

"Retired," he said. His eyes were sunken.

"You'll be back," I said.

He cleared his throat very quietly, as if he were scared of exerting himself too much, which he was, I imagine. Who'd want to cough while clinging to an icy ledge.

"Run them," he said. "Do whatever has to be . . ."

"Basics, Coach. We'll do the basics."

"I said do what you have to. It's your team now." He paused, looked up at the ceiling. "A team. Not some kind of memorial. Take charge."

"Yes, sir," I said.

He closed his eyes. I stood up and left as quietly as possible, feeling like a bull in the chromium shop, and headed back across town to my office in the arena where I ate three dried-up and probably poisonous tunafish sandiwches dispensed from a machine near the locker room, flushing them down with equally poisonous soft drinks. The play-offs— they seemed far off. Not so much in time, which they were, but too far up the mountain for this team. An illusion. Kendall Lea had told me about that guy Sam Johnson who kicked a stone to prove the world was real. How do you kick a mirage?

The sounds of the guys down the hall interrupted my thoughts. They, the guys, were real enough and they were all I had to work with, so I suited up in my yellow and red sweatshirt, took my whistle and my clipboard upstairs and, as I neared the court heard the familiar and—this day— reassuring sounds of basketballs bouncing on the floor and off rims, with the occasional shout or hoot from the players. As I walked down the ramp to the court, watching the casual dance of warm-ups, balls arcing up from several directions, colliding, ricocheting back to the players, the guys ringed around the hoop in a half-circle, effortlessly flipping balls up, I began to feel better. There's a funny echo during practices when the arena is empty, and it usually seems colder, even though all the lights are on. Probably Tub Bligh has the heat turned down.

After a few minutes, I blew the whistle and the balls were

left arcing through the air, colliding, bounding here and there, rolling to a stop, while the team ambled over to me. I told them I'd seen Big Jim, that he looked awful but was in stable condition and would be okay, that Tub Bligh had made me acting coach for the rest of the season, and that it would be announced at a press conference after practice, that they were welcome to attend but, if I were them, I'd avoid it since press conferences are a pain in the ass. They all seemed to agree and practice resumed—basics, working on basic plays, passing, position, picks, a scrimmage with the starters against the rest. They were flat, distracted. I didn't blame them and I wasn't worried. We had another day off before the Portland Trail Blazers came to town and tomorrow would be time enough to get them practicing with intensity. I sent them home early, used the private shower in Jim Munson's office, put on a jacket and tie for press conference. I wondered if I should move into Jim's office, thought it might seem presumptuous, and thought presumptuous to whom? I am the Acting Coach, after all, running the team, and no one else is going to sit in there. Also, it has its own shower, a definite sign of authority and the only perk, in terms of amenities, to be found in the official housing of the team and staff. Tub Bligh thinks about a basketball organization the way he thinks of mining personnel. The coach is semimanagement (thus the shower), the training staff are like low-type foremen (and as assistant coach I was lumped in with the training staff showerwise) and the players are laborers, never mind that these twelve laborers were probably paid as much as all the proles in the Sandia mines. Tub Bligh just doesn't really know what the hell goes on in a basketball organization, and just as well, I guess.

He does know about press conferences. Down a corridor

that seems a half-mile from the locker room, there is a room with black walls and a little platform at one end, opposite the entrance used by the press. Floodlights point at the platform and overhead lights are turned on to let the reporters find seats. Behind the platform is a ten-foot wide nylon Demons banner that Tub personally commissioned from some lady in North Carolina. Once the print guys are in the room, after the local TV guys have set up, the overhead lights are turned off by one of Tub's flunkies from the PR department, the floods kept on, making the banner nearly luminescent, and then, from a door next to the platform, in walks Tub Bligh, on this occasion followed by yours truly, blinded by the floods and the TV lights.

There was a murmur, a tiny bit of perfunctory applause, as Tub stepped up to the standing microphone looking serious.

"Ladies and gentlemen, I have sorry news. The coach of the Demons is out, certainly for the season. He is resting comfortably after suffering a severe myocardial infarction. He will, I'm assured, recover and will be able to lead a normal life, but it will certainly be some time before we know he can resume the abnormal life of a basketball coach. We all pray for him.

"In the meantime," and he smiled, "I need not introduce you to this man, our new Acting Coach, and I mean that with capital letters. He is now in complete charge of the team for the duration of the season. He will bring continuity and energy and the same careful attention to basics that have gotten this team on the move again."

Flashbulbs. I was blinded and hit the mike stand with my hand when I reached for it. It teetered and righted itself.

"A little nervous?" came a voice from the gloom. I was still seeing red after-images of flashbulbs.

"Who, me?" I said. "I'm not nervous. I just can't see. Now I know what it's like to be a ref."

Laughter.

"I'm honored," I went on, "to have Mr. Bligh's trust. I just wish the circumstances were different. We're going to try to carry through Coach Munson's strategy for this season. We've got great guys on this team, and half the season ahead to prove how good we are. It's a tough season and we're going to play hard, just as if Coach Munson were sitting right there on the bench. We'll all do our damnedest. Thanks, guys." I stepped away from the mike.

"Hey, Coach," came a voice from the dark. "You foresee any changes?"

"Changes?"

"Like in the starting line-up, like floor tactics?"

"Nope. We play a basic, fundamental game. No tricks. It's working for us. We'll keep at it."

Another voice: "What are your chances of making the play-offs?"

"Is that you, Dumfrey?" I asked with my most boyish, winning smile. "Dumfrey, I don't do odds, I do basketball. That's all we do here—just basketball. Our job now is to get ready for Portland. They're a tough team with an excellent fastbreak offense. We have to play super defense. Portland is my only concern today. One game at a time. If we execute right all season, we've got a chance—and so does every other team in the league."

Another voice: "Hey, Coach, is that what Kendall Lea does—basketball?"

Oh God, I thought to myself.

"Everyone on the coaching and training staff is here to see to it that our twelve players do their best as individuals and as a team. Does that answer your question?" And before the murmur of negatives grew, I said: "Look, you guys,

I've got to run. I've got a lot of work to do, being the new kid on the block."

"Thank you, ladies and gentlemen," boomed Tub Bligh and we stepped off the platform, out the door, and into the dimly lit corridor.

"Well done," said Tub. "And good luck, son." He shook my hand and headed for the exit, no doubt thinking now about molybdenum.

When I got back to the apartment, it was six-thirty and a garish orange sunset had turned into the last bruise of the day. I was suddenly tired and fumbled with the key in the lock. When I got the door open, I felt better. Kendall Lea was in the kitchen, wearing a long, lavender housecoat, or whatever you call those things, and her blond hair was wet from a shower. She turned and smiled, holding a glass of Scotch and ice.

"You were wonderful," she said and kissed me on the mouth.

"Huh?" I said.

"On the TV. I saw the press conference," she grinned. "I guess I'll have to call you Sir now."

I took the Scotch from her and said: "In your case, it's Snookums."

"Sir is better," she giggled. She folded her legs under her as she sat down on the sofa.

"That lavender looks nice with all those ferns," I said, sitting down beside her. "I'm bushed."

"Me too."

"It's been a long two days."

She tilted her head toward me, like some kind of bird, looking at me obliquely. She does that a lot, peering at me with her head cocked, and it always makes me smile and wonder what she's thinking.

"I got you a present to celebrate your new status," she

said. "I'll get it." She popped off the sofa into the bedroom and came back with a small rectangular package. She sat down and handed it o me.

"Open it," she said, eyes dazzling like a kid. I did, and out of the slim little jewelry store box fell a fairly heavy gold chain.

"Wow," I said. "Thanks. A gold chain."

"It's for your pocket watch," she said.

"Oh. Uh, I don't have . . . uh . . ."

"Yes, you do." She reached into the pocket of her lavender robe and handed me a heavy, reddish-gold watch—it was thin, with Roman numerals on its face. It looked like an antique.

"Holy shit!" I said eloquently. "This is magnificent! Where—I mean it's old, isn't it?"

"It was my grandfather's. He didn't have any grandsons so he gave it to me. He always wore it on big occasions. He would pull it out and study it and he seemed the most important, the wisest man in the world. It was like a symbol of office. So I thought that now you're boss man around here, you should wear it. Let 'em all know who's in charge."

She grinned.

"Sir," she added.

That's how it goes on some days in the NBA.

11 THEY TALK in the sports pages and on the TV about home-court advantage and there is one. All courts fit the regulations for size, basket height, and all that, of course, but no court has exactly the same configuration of wood, lines, color, lights—each is a slightly different environment. If you play half your games and do most of your practicing in one environment, you are at a slight advantage there over some alien. You get to feel at home with how hard the rim is, how the ball will bounce off it. The differences are subtle, but the differences in winning or losing a game are also sometimes subtle. The home-court advantage is something like a dog fighting at home rather than out in the street. It's a real edge, though a big enough dog wins anywhere.

There's a lot of romance about the advantage of playing in front of your own fans. I don't think there's much scientific work that's been done on this one. Hell, we lost to the Nets in New Jersey and their fans are so few and so quiet that it's like playing in a church Tuesday morning. On the other hand, I had the feeling once that the Washington fans woke the Bullets up in the third quarter against us, and they played real ball instead of sleepwalking. But I can tell you something about the fans in Albuquerque. In my first game as acting coach, the fans got the Portland Trail Blazers so off balance they nearly gave up in despair early in the fourth quarter.

It had to do with a University of New Mexico music professor named Jan Alvoord, a classical pianist who shares my belief that NBA basketball is an art form. He's at every home game, win or lose, balding, with thick glasses, and a red mustache over an absurdly phoney, toothy grin. He has a season ticket seat behind the bench, a few boxes away from Taxbreak's, and though I've never met him, he always tries to catch my eye, and wave in a jerky way, and say something like this through his clenched teeth: "Hey, *hey*, coach, doin' good, hey, *hey*." The world is full of nuts.

Anyway, I'm getting ahead of myself. It's on record that we beat Portland that night so I'm not telling you anything you couldn't look up, but I really should tell you about what Kendall Lea said to me the morning after she gave me her grandfather's watch. We were sitting in the morning sun that streamed through the eastern window, through the asparagus fern, onto the kitchen table. Kendall Lea was sitting dreamily, hair unbrushed, elbows on the table, staring at her eggs over easy, bacon, and beer. She had never looked more beautiful—still sleepy, smiling a distant, girlish, silly smile. Move over, Mona Lisa, I thought, you just lost the race.

"You look nice," I said.

"Thank you, sir."

"Hey. It's Snookums, remember?"

She put her hands together, long fingers intertwined. I thought of Tub Bligh making a cathedral out of his hands. Kendall Lea's was prettier.

"I made a mistake," she said.

"A mistake? When?"

"Last December in Portland."

"Like what?" I asked.

"Fred Spokes is a guard," she said.

"No, no, babe, he's a forward. Small forward . . ."

"I know, I know," she said. "He's playing small forward but you were right in Portland when I first met you and you were thinking about moving him to guard. I said it wouldn't work, and it probably wouldn't then, but now he's the best shooting guard you've got." She laughed quietly to herself.

"But Freddy's never played anything but forward. He's too . . ."

"Typecasting," said Kendall Lea. "Everybody believed him when he said he was a forward. Looks like a forward, walks like a forward, quacks like a forward. Must be a forward. Right?" She took a piece of bacon in her fingers and nibbled it. "He's a guard. He knows that now."

I stood up and went to the refrigerator, opened the door, closed it, and returned to my seat at the table.

"Can I ask you a question?" I asked.

"Mm-hmm." Kendall was sawing the egg yolk out of her remaining fried egg, and pushed the egg whites aside. "Hate egg whites. They're . . . well, icky."

"Um, Kendall, why does Fast Fred now think he's an NBA shooting guard?" I tried to sound casual. The sun suddenly rose high enough to make its light vanish from the table.

"The season is getting on, sir, and . . ."

"Will you stop that?"

"Okay, sweetums, the season is getting on, so I figured I better go fast. So I ran a number on Fred. I told him a story, a metaphorical story. He was in a trance, a deep trance, and I told him a story about a mockingbird."

"A mockingbird," I said coolly.

"Right, a mockingbird. It defends its territory like a maniac. Sings like Nat King Cole. In my story the mockingbird defended his territory against a whole bunch of different kinds of hawks, and sang too."

I took a long pull from my Coors.

"You know," I said at length, "Nat King Cole is dead. Fred probably grew up on Jimmy Rodgers."

"Right. But Cole's estate released records of his after he was dead. He lived on, see? Freddy's mother used to play Nat King Cole all day while she did ironing for other people. Immortality. Fred's into immortality. He's your starting guard. That is," she smiled at once dreamily and mischievously, "if it seems right to you, Sir Scrumptious."

Later, on the way to the arena, I stopped at a traffic light and turned to Kendall Lea, whose white silk blouse was embellished with a bright pink silk scarf.

"So who plays in Fred's spot?"

"Del Babbitt."

"He's a *center*. He's seven feet tall."

"But he's a weak center," said Kendall Lea. "We already talked about that. He plays like a weak-side forward. What's the matter with a front line that averages six-eleven?"

I accelerated, barely aware of the boot emporiums and furniture stores passing by.

"And he is ready for that suggestion?"

"Who, Del?"

"Yeah, Del."

She looked out the window with that smile that means there is definitely a joke lying in its lair, about to pounce.

"Most likely," she said, and I didn't want to know what story she had told *that* easygoing geek. Birds? Jesus, this is crazy.

You may have gathered that basketball people are basically conservative. New things tend to freak them out. If a coach all of a sudden announces a change in basic strategy, like a new emphasis on defense, the players say they're having a hell of a time adjusting to the coach's revolutionary new system, and they blow eight games in a row while the Dumfrey Schwartzes all say either: 1. that the coach is a genius, a man of the eighties, and the players are selfish; or 2. that the coach is living in the 1950s and can't handle the New Players of the eighties. You like to introduce any new thing, like a line-up change, gradually, lest you get blamed for everything from a sprained ankle to a mechanical failure in the Nautilus machine.

Knowing all this full well, I nevertheless mentioned to Del Babbitt at practice that I might need him in the late part of the game against Portland as a forward.

"Sure," he said. "But who'll play center?"

"Mo Flynn, if he hasn't fouled out."

"Great, coach," said Del. "That could be real interesting." I tried to figure out if Kendall Lea had turned him into a peregrine falcon, or maybe a Venus flytrap.

Later I motioned to Fast Fred Spokes. He was practicing foul shots. In practice, he is an 88 percent foul shooter, mising only 12 out of 100. In games, this falls off slightly to about 85 percent, still very good. The problem was that Fred avoided contact and got few fouls, so the Demons were missing a lot of points. He loped up to me.

"Hey, man, congratulations, haven't had time to say that yet." He was awash in sweat, an ebony Niagara, glistening in the lights. Balls were thunking on the floor and huge men were leaping and grunting, doing drills. Fast Fred seemed thin, vulnerable.

"Fred," I said. "You're one of the best shooters I've ever seen. I tell people that basketball is American ballet and I point to you."

Fred Spokes beamed.

"Hey, Coach, hey, gee."

"How tough are you, Fred?"

He put his hands on his hips. "Is this more of the rebound rap?"

"Are you tough-minded enough to change positions?" I asked him.

"Hey, look, man, I'm not big enough to . . ."

"Guard. Shooting guard, Fred. Late in the Portland game I want you to pull a switch. I want to shake people up a little and get you scoring as high as you should—and can."

Fast Fred grinned.

"I want you to score. Think about it. Think about Del in your place and you at shooting guard. We're not even going to practice it today. Just think, Fred. You could be the next Ice Man. You could laugh at them all. You could be the Mockingbird."

Fred's eyes darted back and forth like Groucho Marx's. Then he looked at me with the expression you'd expect from a banker you just asked for a loan.

"You're serious," he said.

"Right."

"I think you know what you're doing. Let's try it." He loped off and grabbed a ball, dribbled twice, pulled up and faked a jump shot, throwing the ball at Raphael Flint who was doing nothing much at the time. "Dunk it, you big dummy," Fred shouted. "I want an assist!"

So Portland came into town, I think it was a Friday, you lose track. They're big and fast. We played our usual scrappy, ugly game and we were down only by nine points when the guys were lolling around the locker room at halftime and I said: "We're going to try something new."

They all looked up at me, sweaty brows, suspicious eyes, all but Del Babbitt and Fast Fred. The new line-up would not be evident until after the tip-off beginning the third quarter. But then, at the first whistle, we would change. I gave a few technical instructions and we went back onto the floor.

Now I've got to take you back to Jan Alvoord the music professor. Albuquerque isn't that big a city—around 500,000, about the same as Portland. So oddballs get known faster here than in, say, Philadelphia. This Alvoord was a flamboyant guy, obviously good copy, and he'd been picked up a few times by the local television in their Demon broadcasts as an eccentric fan. So after the night when Jim Munson had keeled over and the fans had picked up on the phrase, Demon State, and had almost brought the house down with the noise, the local TV had gone after Jan Alvoord. The night before the Portland game, Kendall Lea and I had sat watching the late news and they interviewed him.

"Well, Ralph," Alvoord said through his clenched teeth and wide grin, "I think it's a great breakthrough. As a musician, I believe it to be a truly great chant, a kind of ritual, the sort of thing that can make us all closer as a community." Alvoord, crossed his hands over his stomach professorially.

"In fact, I have a thought, Ralph. I'd like to give Demon fans a little lesson in harmonics."

"Well, Mr. Alvoord . . . uh . . ." said Ralph.

The professor grinned and held up his hand. "It won't take more than a second or two. Now listen." He raised his left hand like a symphony conductor. "Deeeeeeeeeee-mon-staaaaaaaaaate," he intoned. "Everybody at home. Deeeeee-mon-staaaaaaaaaate. Good. That was in a major key. Now, try this. DEEEEEEeee-mon-staaaaaaaaaate. You see, that's in a minor key. Suppose everyone in the eastern end of the arena said it in the major key," and he repeated the chant.

"And then everyone on the western end said the minor," and again he chanted. "Dynamite, eh? I'll be in my usual box tomorrow. Let's see what happens. Thanks, Ralph."

Bewildered, Ralph signed off, while Alvoord stood by grinning, a clenched fist raised, and Kendall Lea clutched her stomach and rolled off the sofa to the floor and heaved with silent laughter.

"Oh my God, sir," she finally said. "I think you guys are on a roll."

"Call me Sharkums," I said.

So, it was the beginning of the third quarter with the Demons down by nine. After about four minutes there was a foul, and I sent in the new line-up with a front line averaging six-eleven and Fast Fred in the backcourt and Raphael glowering deeply so as not to reveal his amusement by a mere near-glare, and the Portland players looked desperately at their bench, mutely asking their coach what the hell this was, and we scored eight straight points before they called a time out. By the end of the third quarter we were tied. The guys sat around on the bench, wiping their brows, and looking happy. I showed them a couple of diagrams and while I was explaining something, a spotlight burst on, flooding the boxes behind the bench. Jan Alvoord stood up, with his awful smile, raised his left hand and pointed to the east end of the arena.

"DEEEEEEEEEEEEE-mon-STAAAAAAAAAATE!" (Major)

Alvoord pointed to the west.

"DEEEEEEEEEEEEE-mon-STAAAAAAAAAATE!" (Minor)

It began to echo, and blend, to reverberate into a long weird harmonious maniacal wail over which nothing else could be heard, and they kept it up practically full time until the Blazers walked off the court shaking their heads, losers by ten points, and then it turned into a nearly unbearable roar of approval.

I took out my gold watch and checked the time, which I immediately forgot, put the watch back in my pocket and started off the court after the team. I felt a swat on my fanny, the kind players give each other. I turned and it was Kendall Lea, in her pink silk blouse, the one she had worn at Moriarity's in Portland. She was still sitting on the bench.

"Nice game, coach," she said.

"Basics," I said. "Basics."

So was it brilliant coaching or the intervention of the fans that won the game?

12 THE NEXT MORNING Kendall Lea had an appointment with Isaiah Jones. Ten-thirty at the arena. At breakfast I asked her if it would be all right if I were present in some way.

"Why do you want to be there?" she asked.

"I don't want to breach ethics or anything," I said, "but I'd like to be around. Isaiah is weird these days. I mean, he's not a very nice man."

"You fear for my life?" she said, hands clasped to to her breast. "Oh, Lochinvar."

"I just . . ."

"No, it's fine with me," she laughed. "I don't think he ought to know you're around though."

"Isn't that cheating?"

"Uh-uh. No problem."

So at ten-thirty I was sitting high above the court in one of the VIP boxes—plush seats and a wet bar—when Kendall Lea, dressed in a dark blue sweatsuit, came down the ramp accompanied by a sullen-looking point guard. Except for the three of us, the vast vaulted place was as empty as a monumental tomb. They looked small down there and I wondered why the hell a VIP would want to sit so far from the action. You've really got to sit at floor level or you don't see the game right. Of course I couldn't hear anything the two said but Kendall Lea filled me in later.

Smiling brightly, Kendall Lea walked down the ramp, gesticulating with one hand as she talked to the sulking guard.

"See, Isaiah, you strike me as a man who expresses himself through actions more than words, so I thought if I'm going to get to know you—and I want to get to know you very much—it would help me a lot if I got some firsthand experience of what you do."

Isaiah said nothing and pulled to stop by the bench, head cocked.

"I mean," Kendall Lea went on, "I know what you do as point guard but I'd like to get a feel for it, you know, on the floor. This is all so new for me."

Isaiah was silent, clearly listening for sneak words like "scratch" and "balls."

"You don't need to pull a number on me," he said. "You *can't* pull a number on me. I'm ahead of you."

"Oh, I'm sure of that," she answered, and picked up a basketball from a canvas bin with wheels. She tossed it to him. "Here." Isaiah caught it in his deft hands and looked at her the way a cobra probably looks at a mongoose. "I don't see how you guys can dribble the ball without looking at it. It's amazing."

"You get a feel for it or you don't."

"Could you show me?"

"Why should I? The coach says if I beat you I get $500."

"And if you don't beat me?"

"He gets $500." Isaiah smiled at the absurdity of such an idea.

"Give me a break, Isaiah. I'm not out here to beat you—or to lose to you. That rascal coach—wait till I get my hands on him. Let me ask you, what does a defender look at when you're coming down court?"

"The eyes and the hips." Isaiah absent-mindedly began to dribble the ball.

"Both? That's a tall order."

"It's all in peripheral vision," said Isaiah. "You got to see wide."

Kendall Lea smiled girlishly. "Oh good. Women generally have better peripheral vision than men. See? I have a chance."

"At what?" the guard said.

"To learn this stuff."

Realizing with the arrogance of the superb athlete that he had absolutely nothing to lose, he flipped her the ball and took another from the bin. "Like this, see." He began showing her how to dribble, using the fingertips, how to bend the knees just enough, and all that. He did it slowly and she tried to do the same, making expectable screw ups, losing the ball, and laughing uproariously. From my vantage point it looked like a tiny puppet and an only slightly larger puppeteer. After some ten minutes, while they just stood there facing each other, dribbling the ball, Kendall Lea began to get the hang of it.

"Don't bounce it so hard. Take it easy. Just the fingertips."

Bounce, bounce, bounce.

"Just let it go down easy. It's gonna come back up."

They were face to face, both crouched over, heads up, looking at each other, and then the goddamnest thing happened. They both stopped dribbling the balls. They stood, stooped and facing each other like a couple of broken marionettes, stopped in action, while the two balls stopped bouncing and came to rest. They just stood there for what seemed ten minutes.

Kendall Lea explained afterward what had happened.

"I had to do it nonverbally and covertly."

"What the hell does that mean?"

"It means I had to get him into a trance without using words—he was on the lookout for that—and I had to do it secretively because he didn't want to cooperate. So I got him showing me how to dribble the ball. I was no good so he had to slow down. He had to concentrate his conscious mind on things he usually does unconsciously. So he was—how would you say it—out of his element. I got good enough to match his rhythm. Everything he did I did, like a mirror image."

"And . . .?"

"Then I started breathing at the same rate as his. I blinked when he blinked, and I slowed my breathing down and he was locked into it and slowed *his* breathing down. Then we went off in trances."

"Both of you?" I asked.

"Yes, that's how it works. But mine's different. I can get out of mine myself."

"Oh," I said. Both in a trance. This is loony. "So what then?"

Kendall Lea smiled. "I told him to enjoy his trance, that he would feel refreshed by it, and that he would look forward to his next trance experience, even ask for it. Then I brought him out of it."

That's what it had looked like—stop-action film, the two marionettes staring at each other in a crouch. Then the film began again. They picked up their basketballs, Kendall tossed hers in the bin, and made as if to defend against Isaiah. There were a few jitter steps, a head fake, and Isaiah streaked around her for the lay-up. I could hear her laughing from way up in the VIP box.

Now I looked across the desk at her, still in her blue sweatsuit, one knee drawn up with a sneakered heel propped on the edge of the seat. She smiled that weird smile and said: "So you owe him $500."

"*What?* Look you got *him* in a trance, for chrissake! *You* won."

"Yes, but he beat me at *his* game. That was the bet you made, you scoundrel. So pay."

Jesus. Some kind of lawyer, I thought. Well, it was worth it if Isaiah got consistent. With him playing his game every night and, if the other changes worked out, we damn well could make the play-offs. And if we made the play-offs, and if Tub Bligh's word was good, which I supposed it was, then I'd be the youngest head coach in the NBA.

Kendall Lea broke my reverie: "What are you thinking about?"

"Oh, uh, I was thinking that Tub Bligh said if we made the play-offs I'd be named head coach."

"Is that important?"

"Well, sure, of course it is."

She stood up and put her hands on my desk. Her sapphire eyes gleamed.

"Listen, I gave you my grandfather's watch because you are a big and important man, like he was. I love you and I believe you are a big person. And I came here to try to help you guys get in the play-offs because getting there would remind everyone, the guys, the people out there who pay attention, about human excellence. Human excellence. I don't care about anyone's pride, or greed, or even career. I care about self-esteem. It doesn't make any difference what any of us does next year."

I stared at her.

"So what's the matter with being head coach?"

"Nothing," she said. "It's just that my purposes here are not to give anyone bargaining chips for next year's contract negotiations. I'm trying simply to get some people performing at their best. Their inner best. If that makes them *give up* basketball at the end of the season, I don't care."

She leaned across the desk and kissed me. "I love you, sir, and you'd make a cute head coach." She turned to leave. "So, let's go to the play-offs, you for your reasons, me for mine."

"Let's get married and move to Idaho," I said and as she turned into the corridor she kicked a long, blue-clad leg up behind her, like a dancer in a chorus line. A few minutes later, Taxbreak arrived, tapping once on the door jamb and striding in, wearing his designer suit and his megabuck boots, and sat down in front of the desk with his usual boyish grin.

"Congratulations," he said.

"Thanks."

"You're the boss now."

"Yeah."

"How do you like it?"

"I haven't made up my mind yet."

"Said like a true member of management," said Taxbreak with a bark of laughter. "Hey, seriously, I've got something you better know about."

"What, is Tub Bligh going to sell us to Germany instead of molybdenum?"

"No, this is serious. Real serious. You remember Jeris White's knees? They looked like crêpe paper in the X rays, right? Well, Raphael's on the way. I've been monitoring his . . ."

"He hasn't complained."

"No, no. He won't complain. He takes the cortisone shots

without even wincing. He wants to play, set records, and all that shit. You ever had a cortisone shot? It's like a knife in your joint. But he's got the trainers giving him fifty percent more than is technically allowable—or safe."

I looked at Taxbreak. For all his svelte, boyish good looks, for all his one-of-the-boys kidding, he was serious when he was serious.

"And?"

"And he can't take that many minutes anymore. The knees are going."

"They *can't* go now!" I yelled. "Sorry," I said. "It's just that I've got a winning combination out there. I need him for forty minutes a game."

Taxbreak leaned forward. "He'll give them to you. God knows, he'd play the whole game if he could, but finally the knees are going to go. I mean this season. He needs more rest. In fact, I'd recommend you bench him for the next two games. Medical requirement."

By way of calming myself, I tried to count every blasphemous word I knew. Taxbreak interrupted.

"What are you thinking?"

"That's the second time I've been asked that this morning. I was counting swearwords."

"How far did you get?"

"Twenty-two."

"What were you thinking when you were asked the first time?"

I stood up and picked up my jacket from the back of my chair.

"I was thinking about making the play-offs. I'm still thinking about making the play-offs. Taxbreak, we're going to do it this season. And I intend to have Raphael Flint playing in the play-offs. So you nurse him. Nurse him good.

Give me the papers saying he's got to have a four-day lay-off. Hell, we're playing Philadelphia and Boston. Probably lose anyway."

I pulled my gold pocketwatch out, looked at it and said: "We should both talk to him about it. He'll be about as happy as Mount Vesuvius with stomach cramps."

I walked out of the office and heard Taxbreak say: "Sheees! Basketball!"

You don't know the half of it, Taxbreak, I thought.

I had discovered on Jim Munson's calendar that the coach of the Demons was to appear at twelve-thirty that afternoon at the Spanish-American Veterans of Foreign Wars monthly luncheon. Somewhere out on Juan Tabo Boulevard. I had twenty minutes to make it, and I figured I would probably be late.

The Checker's motor sounded a little wheezy. Needs a tune-up, I thought. Damn car always needs a tune-up. Grumble, grumble. I patted the wheel, a trick I'd learned from Kendall Lea who was ever patting her steering wheel on her Cadillac, encouraging it through the bumps and hard times. I wondered if she patted rocks to encourage them to be patient about erosion.

I yearned for Kendall Lea. My nerve ends were begging.

The thought came to mind that maybe I was too dependent on that precious woman. I wondered if my soul was becoming a welfare case, my happiness depending on whether she shined on me. I decided I was totally dependent on just that and I also decided that was okay. I yearned for her to be in the seat next to me. *Yearned.* Do you know what that word really means?

At the luncheon, I ate the exceptionally good Mexican food, accepted the applause when I was enthusiastically introduced as the Head Demon, and began to talk.

"I'm very glad to be here today. There's no one in this room taller than me and I get sick of craning my neck all day when I talk to my ball club."

Laughter. (It always works.)

"I'm also very glad to be here—and be among heroes. Sometimes basketball players are called heroes, but they aren't offering their lives for their countrymen. You have, all of you here, and so I honor you and thank you on behalf of the Demons and all citizens."

I told them about Jim Munson's health, and told them about the line-up changes and how I thought that was going to work, and I told them a few funny stories about the guys. I told them how basketball players were transients, and could be traded any time, but that all the guys had come to think of Albuquerque as home, and were grateful to this veterans' group for all the civic things it did for the city.

"We also feel a special bond with you and the rest of the Spanish-American population here. We haven't been so hot the past couple of years. We're getting better now and I've learned something very important. We were down—way down in last place—and people could look down on us. You people have been looked down on around here in the past. But Spanish-Americans have kept their pride in their way of doing things and you have helped build this city. Well, the Demons have the same secret ingredient as you do. Even when we lose a game or two, we know we'll prevail one day. The secret ingredient—*you* know—is self-esteem. You've had it for centuries. We've got it, too. And we're going to make you proud of us this year. So. Let's go to the play-offs."

They went bananas, shouted Deeeeee-mon-Staaaaate, and all that. You can't beat good fans. Back at the arena I realized I'd forgotten to ask them who the hell Juan Tabo was.

13 JIMMY ALLEN was six-foot-nine, a gawky forward with a lot of elbows and knees and hustle and that was about all. With Mo Flynn playing center for most of each game now, and Del Babbitt at small forward, it was Jimmy Allen who had to come in off the bench when Raphael flagged or when he fouled out. Jimmy was a second-year man who had played his rookie year in Denver, seeing virtually no action there, and had been picked up before this season by Tub Bligh, who traded a low draft choice for him.

Jimmy had played college ball at San Diego State and was one of those guys who have modest talent and usually bang around the NBA for five, six years, sitting on the bench mostly, and then disappear without a trace. Now, with the need to keep Raphael off the floor for more minutes a game, I was going to have to rely more than I liked on Jimmy Allen. Raphael, who played opposite Jimmy in practices, hardly even deigned to use the kid's name, seeing him—with some accuracy if not empathy—as a nameless piece of cannon fodder, a piece of fluff that would sooner rather than later blow away like a dandelion seed, never to be heard from again.

Jimmy had had some minutes this season, usually going in when the game was already decided and things would get sloppy as they do when the outcome is assured one way or the other. He was fast for a big man but, as I said, gawky,

waving his joints around like an eggbeater. A fair reboun-
der. Now I needed more minutes from him, and I felt the
little chain begin to weaken.

I also needed an assistant coach. The reason why teams
have assistant coaches is simply that the coach can't do
everything himself. I couldn't. And now I had to talk to
Raphael about sitting out two games on doctor's orders and
then playing fewer minutes. He was sitting in my office, a
dark giant staring impassively at the wall.

"Did Taxbreak talk to you?" I asked.

"Yeah."

I waited.

"He says the knees are bad."

I waited.

"Look, man, I know my knees are bad. I can feel it, you
know. They hurt. But pain don't bother me. I been playing
in pain for two years, three years." He glared. "But I got
things to do. We're playing real good now and I don't want
to spend a whole lot of time on my ass on the bench."

"Do you think we're playing well enough to make the
play-offs?" I asked.

"Hell, yes."

"Listen, Raphael, I think we've got a good chance to get
there, too. And I want you playing in the play-offs. So I've
got to pace you some—I've got to. Otherwise you could lose
the knees and the team would lose you altogether."

"Well, who the hell is going to play power forward if I'm
sitting on my ass half the time? That Allen kid? He doesn't
know what the hell to do in a real game."

"He's all we've got, Raphael."

"Shit." Part of Raphael's distain for Jimmy Allen was that
Jimmy Allen was listed as a power forward and anyone
anywhere who played power forward was a threat—how-

ever slight—to Raphael's position. He wasn't scared of anyone, but merely pretended that other candidates for his
position didn't exist.

"So I'm telling you that you have to sit out the next two
games and then play less—maybe thirty minutes a game."

The dark giant sat motionlessly, glaring at the wall above
my head.

"Shit," he said presently.

"And," I went on, "you've got to help me with the kid."

"Hey, look, I'm a player. I got my own style, my own
stuff. I don't share that with anyone. I ain't no coach."

"Yes, you are," I said.

"I am what?"

"I need an assistant coach, Raphael. I want you to be the
assistant coach. A playing assistant coach. Want to try it
out?"

Raphael stood up, towering over my desk. He glared.
His forehead shined with a tiny film of perspiration.

"I don't know nothin about coaching, man. I'm a player."

"Look, Raphael, the guys look up to you. You're the elder
statesman around here." I grinned. Raphael frowned.
"They'll listen to you. Suppose I get a bunch of technical
fouls called on me and they throw me out of the game?
Who the hell is going to run things then? I need you,
Raphael."

The big man sat down. "So I'd be on your staff, huh?"

"Right."

"You want an assistant who gets paid more than you do?"

"Everyone gets paid more than I do. There have been
stranger relationships."

"And Kendall Lea, being on the training staff, has to take
orders from me, right?"

"Wrong."

Raphael snorted, his nostrils flared. "Just a joke, boy," he said impassively. "Let me use your phone." He stood up and dialed some numbers with a long dark finger. "Dora? The doctor says I can't play so much anymore. Knees." Silence. "I know, I know. We been over all that. No, I don't like it. Yeah, well, they also want me to be acting assistant coach. What do you think of that?" More silence. "Yeah. Well, okay. I'll see you later." Raphael hung up the phone slowly and carefully. He stared down at me.

"Okay. Assistant coach. Shit." He stuck out his huge hand and I stood up and shook it.

"Thanks, Raphael."

"So what do I do?"

"Turn Jimmy Allen into a player."

Raphael almost smiled. By that I mean that for just a fleeting instant there was a suggestion of a crinkle around his eyes.

"I knew it," he said. "I knew that you were going to get me to help that gawky bastard. I knew it." He turned and walked out of the room.

We let it out to the press that afternoon that Raphael had back spasms and would be out for two games at least. Naturally, we lied about it because we didn't want anyone to imagine just how bad Raphael's knees were. We coupled that announcement with the fact that he was assistant coach, and Raphael submitted—which he rarely did—to an interview.

"When do you assume your new duties, Raphael?" asked Dumfrey Schwartz in the locker room after practice. The big man was sitting on a bench before his locker, pouring copious amounts of sweat through his pores, his wide, thick chest gleaming.

"I already did."

"What are they?" asked Dumfrey.

"Teach everyone on this team my tricks."

"Your tricks, Raphael, what are they?"

"How to be ugly, and mean, and nasty."

Raphael turned toward his locker and the interview was over. Dumfrey turned around in confusion and saw Fast Fred Spokes draped over the water cooler like a bunch of charcoal sticks. Fred, also awash with sweat, grinned broadly at the little reporter.

"Talk to *me*, Dumfrey. I got plenty to tell you, boy. You want to hear my new name?" Dumfrey took out his little notebook. "They call me the Mockingbird now. Got it? The Mockingbird. I can *fly*." And Fred made a swooping motion with his hand. "And I can *sing*. I sing like a mockingbird, a different tune for every occasion." The rest of the guys in the locker room whistled and shouted catcalls and Dumfrey waddled out looking a little disoriented.

I drove home that night feeling that maybe the team was a little bit more than a boat made out of scrap wood held together by Scotch tape. The clowning around in the locker room at Dumfrey's expense had shown spirit, the kind of esprit de corps that had been so lacking in the first part of the season. Things were coming together, maybe—at last. I prayed that between Raphael and Kendall Lea, Jimmy Allen would be at least adequate, good enough to hold up his end while Raphael rested. We were beginning to reach that part of the season where you lose track of games, of cities. The schedule becomes a kaleidoscope of arena after arena, of plays, improvisation, exhaustion. By the end of a season all the teams are playing on sheer instinct. There's no way, no time to think. Just guts and instinct. I wondered, when it got that far along in the season, if these guys had the instincts, if Kendall Lea had truly been able to reach down into the guys' souls enough so their instincts—their true instincts—could carry them through the nightmare. God, I wanted to get to the play-offs. I could taste it.

But we were so thin. Aside from Jimmy Allen and, of course, Green Bay Packer, whom I used as a relief in the backcourt for Fred, putting him in to calm things down when they got a little wild, we had very little usable meat on the bench. Joachim Taylor, who we called Joe-Jim, was the rookie point guard—a slick kid from Baylor, quick and a good shooter but a kid, still too inexperienced to quarterback the team the way a point guard is supposed to. I had been giving him more minutes, and working with him at practice, but he had a tendency to turn the ball over, to throw a bad pass and let the other team get it. One thing you really hate to see is turnovers. In addition, we had two more forwards—nobodies—and one more nobody shooting guard. We were really a team of eight men. It takes more than that, generally speaking, to make the play-offs. Well, I thought, other teams don't have a secret weapon. Kendall Lea had certainly worked wonders on the starting five, maybe she could do some miracles on the others. It could, I thought, be worse.

We would leave early the next morning for Philadelphia, then Boston, then Atlanta—our last eastern road trip, which made me grateful, since the east has the toughest teams overall in the NBA. Kendall Lea and I went out for dinner to The China Hand, the warehousy place on Juan Tabo Boulevard. The maitre d' crinkled up in smiles as we walked in, and pumped my hand and said how happy he was for the Demons, and all that, and showed us to a semicircular booth that could seat four.

"Please," he said with a little bow. "Enjoy yourselves." And he strode off, snapping his fingers at one of the waiters who was standing around. Within minutes, we had tea and drinks on the table and an order in for pot stickers or jounces, whatever the hell it is Kendall Lea calls them.

"It must be nice, being a celebrity," Kendall Lea said with a smile. "Service with a smile and all."

"Maybe," I said, "but I'm tired and I only started this stuff."

"I feel tired, too," she said. I looked over at her. She was wearing her pink silk blouse and had her hair up, fixed behind her head with a silver barrette. She was looking out across the restaurant and, now that I looked at her, I could see little signs of fatigue around her eyes.

"It's going to get worse before it gets better," I said.

"What do you mean?" she asked, looking at me quickly.

I explained about the season, how it piles up on you as you go into the last twenty, thirty games, how by the end everyone is going out there on sheer guts. I told her about how Raphael was now assistant coach and some of the things I had worried about in the car, notably, my hope that between her and Raphael we could get some good minutes out of Jimmy Allen.

She sighed.

"I'm sorry," I said. "I shouldn't be talking shop. We're both tired."

She put her hand on mine and squeezed it in her long fingers.

"You know," she said, deftly snapping up a pot sticker in her chopsticks like a heron after a minnow, "there are some situations where hypnosis can't do anything."

"You've got to be kidding. You've worked miracles on those guys. Look, Raphael is now a team player, Mo is a killer, Fred is flying at guard—and Isaiah, look at him. I think he's probably off the stuff. He's weird as hell still, a loner, but on court he's playing 100 percent. Here, you have that one," I said, referring to the last pot sticker.

"What, and be an old maid?" she smiled.

"Lady, that's about as likely as an egg laying a chicken."

She giggled, and took the pot sticker. She was an enthusiastic eater, in fact, she ate like an athlete, but it never seemed to show up anywhere on her. We explored China Hand's encylopedic menu and I was glad to have gotten off business talk. I realized that I wasn't the only one who was working, and I guessed that putting people in trances was tiring work. After several minutes of decision-making and decision-rescinding, we ordered Moo Shu Pork and Hot and Sour Cabbage. My mother used to make me eat boiled cabbage and I decided that when I was on my own I'd never get within ten feet of cabbage—or beets, which I believe should all be sent back to Russia where they belong—but Chinese cabbage is something altogether different. Doesn't even look like cabbage.

We had another drink while we waited for the main course and Kendall Lea returned to business.

"Isaiah does seem to be a lot steadier now," she said.

"He sure does."

"He's come to me twice now to put him in a trance. He comes into my office and just sits there, making small talk, until I ask him if he wants a session. Then off he goes. He doesn't change expression much, or say much afterwards. Just says thanks and walks off, looking a little embarassed."

I took a sip of my Scotch. "So you don't know where he's going in those trances?"

"Nope. He seems perfectly comfortable."

"Well, if the shoe fits," I said.

The main course arrived, served with silent élan by the obsequious waiter, and we heaped portions of each on our plates, rolling up the pork in those little pancakes.

"The shoe seems to fit," she said, "but it makes me nervous."

"Why?"

"No feedback."

"You don't need feedback, do you? He's playing like a demon."

Kendall Lea ate some cabbage. "This is wonderful!" she said. "No, it makes me nervous when I don't get any idea, any at all, about where he's going, what he's doing in those trances." She put down her chopsticks and leaned toward me. "You see, this stuff I'm doing. It's . . . it's very strong. Powerful. You're dealing with peoples' minds."

"Like brainwashing," I said.

"No, no. Not brainwashing. I don't tell these guys what to think. It's unleashing something, something from their unconscious. Whatever is there to unleash."

I looked in her face and there seemed to be little signs of pain in her expression.

"But," I said, "didn't you tell me that the unconscious mind will protect you. I mean, what harm can come from it?"

She took my hand again. "That's the theory we work on. And it works. But. . . " She looked off across the restaurant.

"But?"

"It's like playing god. It's scary. What if something went wrong? What if I made a mistake?" She squeezed my hand. Like playing god, I thought. Jesus. I hadn't thought of it that way, I hadn't realized what this lady was putting herself through. It must be exhausting every time she worked on someone. It must be terrifying.

"What kind of thing could go wrong?" I asked.

"That's the trouble. I don't know."

"Would you feel better laying off for a while? I mean. . . "

"No, no." She smiled at me, a loving, sad smile I had never seen before. "There are things I have to do here." She squeezed my hand again. "It's okay, I just got a little tired. That's all. Let my guard down for a second."

"You don't have to guard against me," I said. "Anything. . . "

"I love you, sir, and I know that." She smiled a happy smile. "So tell me more about Jimmy Allen. I've talked to him a few times and he seems like a nice guy. Hey, can I have some more pork?"

I told her about Jimmy Allen and the things I hoped he could learn to do on the court—a kind of basketball Berlitz training course—all the while thinking in the back of my mind that if there is such a thing as god, the odds are six to five he's a she.

14 WE LOST TO Philadelphia the next night—in fact, we were blown away before the third quarter ended. Raphael sat next to me on the bench in street clothes—a gray suit with a red tie. He looked like some kind of grouchy executive and I wondered how they ever found enough gray pin-striped flannel to house him. At each break in the game, he took Jimmy Allen aside and talked to him, making fierce little gestures with his hands. The next night we beat Boston— Boston! Can you believe it?—mostly because Mo Flynn had his best night of the year, patrolling the boards like he was the Coast Guard, picking up rebounds he shouldn't have been able to get and scoring 36 points. Isaiah was relentless, bringing the ball down court with a marvelous variety of stutter steps and feints, passing off like a surgeon. He had eighteen assists, his highest of the season.

Two days later we lost in Atlanta. I hate that place. Atlanta doesn't seem capable of fielding a team that isn't all thug. The whole game was played in the trenches, muscle against muscle, a butcher shop. In all, six players fouled out and, with mostly substitutes playing the last few minutes, it looked like street warfare. A coach's nightmare—for both coaches— and we lost by five points, and flew back to Albuquerque, licking our bruises and wounds. Raphael had played two stints adding up to about twenty minutes. His knees, he said, felt better, but the lay-off had made a difference in his timing. These guys aren't machines.

Back in the west, we surged, winning four in a a row, dropping two, winning four more. As the season turned into a phantasmagoria of plane trips, hotels, pick-up practices, fans at home shrieking Deeee-mon-Staaaate like maniacs, muscle and sweat, battles without let up, crummy food, just confusion, we were winning two of every three games and had an insecure hold on third place in our division—good enough to make the play-offs. Mo Flynn was holding up like a circus bear, beating everyone who chose to wrestle. Blue-collar ball from the Ivy-Leaguer, thuggery and hard work. Raphael played his thirty minutes with an intensity you'd expect from a man five years younger. Fast Fred, the Mockingbird, was getting off his graceful shot from all over the court and even playing defense. One night, I think it was in Seattle, he faked a jumpshot and dove in for a lay-up, right over the top of Seattle's center. "In your face!" Fast Fred had said loud enough for everyone within fifty feet to hear. "The Mockingbird sings again!" Del Babbit was drifting around in his area, getting off nice shots, passing well, even getting the occasional rebound. Jimmy Allen didn't make any dumb mistakes, got rebounds, and played defense. It all gets mixed up. In San Diego, the airline lost our luggage, all of it. Can you imagine that, for Chrissakes? We didn't even have uniforms. We had to wear San Diego's away uniforms for the game, which was humiliating. Mo Flynn was sitting in the locker room before the game with his unfamiliar uniform, looking at it sort of quizzically. It was a bit too small for him. "These guys smell worse than even us," he said and the guys went bananas and beat San Diego in their own damn underwear by twelve points.

I woke up one morning comfortably tangled up in Kendall Lea's arms and legs, wondering how we fit together so well when she was ten inches shorter than me, and then wondering where we were—somewhere on the road. She murmured and woke up, pretty as a cat, and said "Where are we?" I got out of bed and looked out the window. It was a dark gray morning and it was raining.

"It's raining. Must be either Portland or Seattle," I said.

"We just played those guys," she said dreamily.

"Yeah, right. Then it's Denver."

Weird things were happening. For example, playing Raphael only thirty minutes a game was the best thing that had happened to him all season. It was better for his knees, and it gave him the rest he needed to play that half-hour like a dervish. We found that when we had to put Joe-Jim, the rookie, in to spell Isaiah, he played with what almost approached assurance if we also put Green Bay Packer in to help him bring the ball down court. At such times we'd move Fred Spokes back to forward, and spell Del Babbitt. Fred would amble up to his new opponent and say: "Watch it, big stuff. You dealin with the Mockingbird now." We didn't get as many points in that configuration, but we didn't fall too far behind, either. Things were clicking at last, although we were all almost too dazed to appreciate it.

One night in Albuquerque, after we had squeaked past Utah—the team is named the Utah Jazz, for god's sake, and that's because they used to be the New Orleans Jazz; I always thought they should have changed their name to something more appropriate like the Utah Tabernacles or something—anyway, we squeaked past Utah and Taxbreak asked me and Kendall Lea if he could buy us a drink.

Taxbreak likes to hang out in one of those really noisy taverns that have popped up in parking lots around Albuquerque, the kind of place where room after room is filled with stuff that's supposed to look like it was imported from some eighteenth-century English pub, and where waitresses in improbable doily-type hats and western twangs serve heavy British beer and lots of beef all day. Maybe it reminds him of the days he hung out in noisy singles bars when he was in med school. I don't know. There's no accounting for taste—especially bad taste.

"They're going to have to start manufacturing a new set of keys to the city," said Taxbreak, after we had gotten our drinks. "It looks like the play-offs, right?"

"Maybe," I said. "San Antonio is right behind us and if we mess up we could go right down the tube."

"So don't mess up."

"Thanks, bone man. You just keep Raphael's knees glued together."

Kendall Lea was sitting quietly, sipping her Canadian whiskey and watching the patrons with a faraway smile. I loved watching her at moments like that. The peace that usually surrounded her almost glowed when she was far off somewhere dreaming. She had on a white blouse with a ruffle at her neck, and had put on a black velvet jacket over that—made her look like a matador. There was some big brass dangly necklace hanging below the ruffle and it caught the orange light from all the little candles in the room and dazzled. I was tired, but it was a good kind of tired.

Taxbreak leaned over, getting Kendall Lea's attention, but spoke to me. "Tell me, what the hell was Isaiah doing in the locker room before the game?"

"What do you mean?" I asked.

"He was in a trance," said Kendall Lea.

"I thought so," said Taxbreak. "You've taught him to do

it himself, right? A light trance that he can get out of by himself?"

"That's right." said Kendall. "He seems to think that if he gets a little quiet moment in a trance before the game that he can concentrate better. He's very adept at it."

"Does that worry you?" asked Taxbreak.

"A little," she said and looked at me. "But I can't come in the locker room and do it for him."

Taxbreak guffawed. "I bet those guys would be proud as peacocks if you came into the locker room. Hey! Miss? Another round here."

Kendall Lea looked at the doctor. "Does it worry you?"

"Nah, hell no. Once an addict, always an addict."

"What are you talking about?" I asked. "He's off that shit, isn't he?"

"Coke? Yeah, he's off it. But he's an addictive personality. Don't you know anything, Coach? He's off coke and he's on trances. Addicts just don't drop something without a substitute. I think it's great. If we could get all the hopheads in the country on hypnosis, the mafia would start taking early retirement."

"I'll be damned," I said. I turned to Kendall. "Was that what you were planning?"

"Not exactly." She stared off into space, and said something that I didn't hear because some burly asshole was laughing at his own joke at the next table.

"What did you say?"

She turned back and looked at me expressionlessly. "I said, I hadn't thought of it just that way."

I felt a tingle on the back of my neck, and the round of drinks arrived and we talked about other things, Taxbreak fooling around and laughing at *his* jokes until the burly guy at the next table started turning around and glowering at us. "Sourpuss," said Taxbreak as we left.

The next night was the seventy-first game we had played that season, the Denver Nuggets, with ten more games to go before the regular season came to an end. It hadn't been a regular season, of course, and by the time Denver was on the plane back home, the word regular had disappeared from my vocabulary. During the Denver game the roof caved in, as if you had been sitting in front of your hearth reading bedtime stories to your toddlers and having a martini and a meteorite plummeted in from outer space and came right through the roof onto your living room rug, and you didn't know for weeks what had really happened except that an unmeasureable disaster had occurred.

It was after the half-time break and we were trailing Denver by five, and I was talking to Raphael while the other guys were shooting balls up in arcs for warmup, and something struck me as wrong. Then I realized what it was.

"Where's Isaiah?" I asked. Raphael glanced around at the team.

"I don't know. I thought he was right behind me when we came out on the court."

"Shit." I said. "You better get back in the locker room and see what's up."

The big man took off at a lope. A few minutes before the buzzer for the third quarter was about to go off, he returned, a look of volcanic fury on his face.

"Sucker's not there. Not in the can. Nowhere. His clothes are gone."

"Goddammit!" I shouted. "Goddammit!" I looked around uselessly at the sea of faces in the arena. "That stupid, goddamn motherfucking creep! Goddamn half is going to start in thirty seconds. Raphael, go tell Joe-Jim he's going to start this half. Don't tell him Isaiah's split or the kid'll piss green."

I went over to the bench in a daze. People were yelling and applauding here and there around the arena, kind of like outbursts of distant gunfire, everyone all revved up to see their beloved Demons pull another game out of the fire and brimstone. Shit.

"What's the matter?" asked Kendall Lea, wide-eyed,

"Isaiah's gone AWOL, that's what the matter is. Fucking little jerk."

"Oh, my god," said Kendall. "I'll go try to call him. Maybe he went home. Maybe he was sick."

"If you get him, tell him to stay put. I want to see him after the game. I don't care if he's got the black fucking plague. Tell him I'm coming to see him. I'll fine the little bastard half his damn salary." The buzzer sounded and Kendall Lea fled up the ramp towards the locker room, and I sat down on the bench, my head filled with my own scream of fury, as the fans applauded and cheered and yelled, "Go, Demons," and the players trotted out onto the court.

Needless to say, we lost. And needless to say, Kendall Lea did not find Isaiah. He hadn't gone home. Or, if he had, he wasn't answering the phone. At the break after the third quarter, the team knew that Isaiah was gone for the night and I had to tell them that I din't know where the hell he was. Raphael played an extra ten minutes that game, and Green Bay did his best to sooth Joe-Jim but it didn't work and we lost by nine points, a game we should have won if that goddam psycho hadn't blown it. Jee-*sus*, that stuff makes you mad.

In the locker room, after the guys had showered and were glumly going about the business of leaving, Joe-Jim came up to me. "Coach?"

"Yeah, Joe-Jim. What is it?"

"I'm sorry. I screwed up out there."

"Yeah, well, you weren't the only one. Don't worry."

"It's one thing, playing out there now if I know that Isaiah can come in. It gives me confidence. . . "

"Look, you're a good basketball player. You can play with the best. Don't worry." I realized that I was not supposed to tell anyone not to worry because, as Kendall Lea had said, it makes them do just that. "Look kid, you may have to take on the starting assignment if we don't find Isaiah. You can handle it. I've been watching you. You're doing okay."

"Thanks, Coach. Uh, Coach?"

"Yeah, what?"

"Isaiah told me a few things early in the season. You know, when he was on the stuff. I think he wanted me to, you know, join him or something. He told me to meet him at some place. I didn't go, you know, I don't want . . . "

"What place? Do you remember the name?"

"Yeah, it was, let's see, it was something like . . . a simple name. It was . . . the Mexican Hat."

"Okay, Joe-Jim, good. Go home and get some rest. Raphael!" I shouted. "Let's go. We got a place to start." We went out into the parking lot where Dora was waiting in a red Cadillac convertible. Raphael explained, and Dora drove off through the sickly blue circles of light, while we headed for my Checker.

The Mexican Hat was a multi-ethnic bar in the midst of what you would call the barrio near the Rio Grande and a mile or so, maybe more, from Old Town Albuquerque, the touristy place you get to be heading west out of town. I felt sick. I was thinking also about Isaiah Jones, jerk that he was, being degraded by hanging out in the Mexican Hat. We pulled up outside.

"Thanks, Raphael."

"Don't thank me, man. We can use that little shit. I'm as mad as you."

Inside, it was expectably dark, a long bar extending back into a reddish gloom, loud stupid music blaring from some machine, loud stupid people weaving in and out of the shadows, Chicanos, Indians, blacks, whites, dregs. A man who makes $250,000 a year has to fool around in here? I thought. We went up to an open place at the bar and the little Mexican barkeep, wearing tight black pants and a white shirt, turned toward us.

"Hey, aren't you Raphael Flint?" People near us at the bar turned and looked up at the giant in their midst. Raphael leaned across the bar and the little man minced over in his tight pants. "What can I get you? Hey, wow. A celeb."

There was a little pocket of silence around us amidst the drone of the place. Raphael leaned farther across the bar and looked expressionlessly at the barkeep.

"You know Isaiah Jones?"

The barkeep smirked. "Sure, I know Isaiah."

Suddenly the barkeep was off the ground, his groin resting on the edge of the bar, his feet dangling down among the dirty glasses, his throat in the big right hand of the Demons' gigantic power forward. Raphael spoke through big white clenched teeth, looking like some kind of predatory animal from thousands of years ago.

"I don't want to waste any time in this crud hole, boy." said Raphael in his high voice that sounded like the song of a python. "Where do I find my teammate tonight?" The little man glugged.

"He hasn't been in here for . . . "

The little man shook like a rat in the claws of a big cat.

"Hey, I'm serious. He hasn't been here for weeks . . . "

And Raphael said. "Now *you* know there is a big mirror behind you, don't you, greasehead? And *you* know when I throw you into that mirror it's going to break into a million little pointed slivers and most of them are going to find their way into your greasy body. I'm going to do that unless you tell me where I can find Isaiah tonight. You hear me, dipshit?"

"I swear to the Sacred Mother he hasn't been in here for weeks." The barkeep jerked as Raphael began to haul him over the top of the bar. People were standing back, smiling, loving it, and a silence had fallen over the entire place. The barkeep was blubbering, gasping, clutching the enormous forearm from which he was suspended.

Raphael spoke loudly, turning to the crowd. His usually high voice had the timber of an operatic tenor.

"If I don't hear where I can find Isaiah Jones," he said in measured words, "then this man here is going to intensive care." There were a lot of shouting and cheers. "Wring his neck." "Who cares?"

"And," Raphael intoned, "he's gonna be the first of you little people to bleed. Now WHERE do I find Isaiah Jones?" He shook the barkeep. A voice came out of the reddish gloom, a heavily laden Mexican accent.

"He would come here and then go to the Orange Rooster."

Raphael glared into the dark where the voice had been. "You better be right, motherfucker, or I'm coming back here and cut your damn eyes out of your head." He dropped the barkeep, who collapsed behind the bar along with what seemed most of the glassware, and glared left to right in a

180-degree catch-all statement. And then we walked out of the Mexican Hat.

It all seemed red lights that night, the worst parts of Albuquerque, sleaze bars, guys looking progressively more lost and stupid, drunk and doped, in the shadows, more obsequious when Raphael pushed someone four feet up a wall.

"The only good offense is offense," said Raphael between two dives. "We'll find the little shit." I was very glad Raphael was on my side. In one place, a great big flabby Navajo Indian said something wrong and found himself, squealing in fear, hanging on a peg on the wall from his jacket collar while Raphael explained that it had been black cavalrymen a century ago who had turned the Navajo tribe into a bunch of bedwetters and they had a right still to be scared of blacks.

I had never seen anything like it. Raphael was like some ebony Titan, terrorizing people not only with his size but his race. Being around basketball so much I didn't really pay much attention to color but I realized that here in the Southwest, blacks were relatively few, and blacks did have a history of being fierce cavalrymen long ago when the place was being made safe for the white man. Mexicans and Indians were suspicious and even downright scared of blacks, a kind of racial memory. So were whites. Especially scared of blacks who were six-ten and mad.

In one disgusting dive, after Raphael made it clear what he had in mind, he turned to the bartender and said in a loud voice: "Hey, boy, you better tell them wetbacks over there—the ones with their hands in their pockets?—that one street nigger from the north like me knows more about knives than the whole Mexican army." The Mexicans took their hands out of their pockets.

We found Isaiah at about three in the morning hunched

over in a chair in the back of a nameless dive, his legs splayed out before him, fancy boots toes up. A girl with a big ass flitted away as Raphael approached like some figure out of mythology.

"Hey, asshole," said Raphael in an altogether surprisingly gentle voice. "You're in the wrong place again. Let's go home."

Isaiah nodded and drooped farther into the chair he was sitting on. "Yeah," he said. "Carry me back to Ole Virginny. I knew a virgin once. Big tits. Hey, want some coke?"

Raphael reached out one of his big hands and pulled the little guard's face up. Even in the dim light, his eyes were bloodshot bruises. Yellow gunk was in his eyes. He was sweating. "Isaiah," said Raphael, "Isaiah. You're coming with me, now."

"Un-unh. Staying here."

"No, man, we're going home."

Isaiah shook his head. "Don' wanna go home. No, stay here. Hey." He looked up, a stupid grin allowing white teeth to shine. His eyes flickered back and forth. "Hey, Rafe, hey, man, let's go to the All Star game anyway, surprise the fuckers." His head sagged. Raphael picked him up and slung him over his shoulder. He faced the crowd of jerks that had gathered at the deep end of the bar in silence. "You . . . " he said. He looked like a volcano about to explode. And then, in his soft, high voice, he said: "I've seen scummier people than you. Somewhere, I know I've seen scummier people than you." And he walked out of the bar with Isaiah Jones across his shoulders, an African god, a Detroit street thug who knew more about everything than anyone in the world. No one said a word as we left.

15 RAPHAEL sat beside me in the Checker, the lights of the fast-food joints and bars and gas stations and all-night grocery stores reflecting from the whites of his eyes. He was turned sideways, a long arm on the seat back, watching the dark heap in the backseat that was Isaiah Jones, point guard.

"He's blown his brains on the stuff," Raphael said. "Even if he comes out of it, he's lost half his damn brains. He's finished."

"We're almost to his place," I said. "I'll call Taxbreak."

Isaiah lived in a place a lot like mine—a long two-story building of white stucco and wrought-iron railings and oaken doors. Raphael fished the keys out of Isaiah's pocket, hoisted him on his shoulder and went up the stairs. A yellow light bulb was on outside Isaiah's apartment. We went in, flipped on the lights and I headed for the phone, while Raphael set Isaiah down in an easy chair.

After four rings, Taxbreak answered sleepily.

"Taxbreak. It's me. Isaiah went AWOL at half time. Raphael and I found him in some dive. He looks like he may have O.D.'d"

"Where are you?"

"At Isaiah's place."

"I know where it is. I'll be there in driving time." He hung up. Raphael was wiping Isaiah's face with a wet dish towel.

"Get a blanket. We got to keep him awake and warm."

I found a blanket in the bedroom and brought it in. Raphael wrapped it around Isaiah. The little guard sat, his hands on his thighs, his head back. "Isaiah?" said Raphael. "Isaiah. You stay awake. Can you hear me?"

"I don't want to be here." Isaiah said.

"Where do you want to be, boy?"

"Let's go to the Mexican Hat."

"You're home, man. You'll be okay."

"No." He began breathing slowly and deeply and closed his eyes.

"Don't go to sleep, man, wake up." said Raphael. "Shit, we don't want him to go to sleep."

I looked at Isaiah. His face was sickly pale behind the color. Under his eyelids, his eyeballs moved back and forth. He breathed slowly, strongly.

"He's not asleep, Raphael. I think he's put himself in a goddamn trance."

"What do we do?" asked the big man. "How do we get him out? Shit, man, this is dangerous."

He turned and reached down with the wet towel. Suddenly, Isaiah lurched violently, his head jerking to one side, as if he'd been hit. Raphael drew back, wide-eyed.

"What, did you hit him?" I asked.

"Didn't touch him."

Isaiah lifted one arm up, as if to shield himself from other blows, and made a sound like a cough, and then another, and another, as if he were trying to talk. "Baay . . . " He doubled over, hands over his head and coughed: "Baaay . . . baaaay. No. Baaaaay." Then he shouted. "No! Baby, No! baby!" It was a woman's voice. "No, Billy, Billy, no! Baby!"

The hairs stood up on the back of my neck. Raphael drew

back another step, looking wide-eyed at the little heap that had been Isaiah. "Shit," he said. Isaiah jerked sideways, as if struck again. "No, Billy, don't!" shrieked the woman's voice. Isaiah crumbled to the floor, weeping woman's sobs, scuttled a few feet, and got to his feet, his hands over his stomach. "The baby, Billy! Don't!" Isaiah reeled under another blow. The woman screamed again, a long, hysterical wail, "Don't don't! Don't let Baby Isaiah see! Oh God!"

Isaiah reeled and jerked under a rain of blows, the woman's voice shrieking, and then was hurled backwards into the bathroom door. It slammed open and Isaiah fell through it backwards and there was a sickening thunk, like a melon falling from a high place onto a floor.

"Holy shit." I said. Raphael and I stood motionless.

"I ain't going in there," said Raphael, his eyes about bugged out of their sockets. I went into the bathroom and Isaiah was lying on the tiled floor, his head at an awful angle. I put my ear to his chest, and tried with my right hand to find a pulse. No pulse. No heartbeat.

"Jesus, he's dead." I got up. "Raphael, for Chrissakes, he's dead!"

Raphael was standing in the same place, his eyes wide. "He was killed," said the big man.

"What the hell are you talking about?"

"He was killed."

"Come on, there was no one here but you and me. And him."

"What was that voice then?" asked Raphael, still standing as still as a rock. "Who was that woman's voice?"

"He went bananas. Hysterical. Too much dope. I don't know, for Chrissakes!"

The front door opened and Taxbreak burst in.

"Where is he?"

"In there," I said. "He's dead."

Taxbreak bolted into the bathroom and bent over the limp figure on the floor. His hands moved over the body, pausing now and then. He lifted up Isaiah's head and peered at the back of his skull. Then he stood up. "He's dead all right. Blow to the head. What happened?"

I told him exactly what had happened, from the time we found him until he went into the fit, shrieking like a woman about the baby, and then, as if he's been punched, fell into the bathroom through the door.

"I'll call the police," said Taxbreak. "You guys get yourselves a drink. Get me one, too. Then sit down."

Raphael was standing in the same position, motionless. "I don't want no drink. Who was that woman's voice, man? Who?"

Taxbreak hung up the phone. "They'll be here in a few minutes. You're going to have to tell them everything. But tell them only what you know you know. You don't really know if he was in a hypnotic trance before he went bananas, so you don't have to mention that. Okay? He was obviously flooded with booze and cocaine, that's enough to explain it. Raphael, sit down." The big man lowered himself absently into a chair.

"I wonder who that woman was," he said, staring at the chair where Isaiah had sat. Taxbreak looked at Raphael sharply, then looked away, and took a big sip of Scotch.

The cops came in a few minutes, a plainsclothes sergeant and a patrolman. We told them what had happened. They asked us again and again about the bizarre fit Isaiah had been in before he fell in the bathroom. "And you guys just stood there while he was lurching around? I would have thought a couple of basketball players would have the reflexes to stop a man from doing that."

"Look, sergeant," interrupted Taxbreak, "these guys have basketball player's reflexes. They don't deal with head-cases. Some coke-head goes into a violent fit like that, most people I know would be too surprised, too shocked to react."

"It happened awfully fast, sergeant," I said. "He all of a sudden started lurching around and—crash—went through the door."

"Yeah, yeah, I suppose so," said the sergeant. "Okay, you guys can go. We'll take care of this." He indicated the bathroom with his head. "You'll be around tomorrow?"

"Yeah. We're scheduled to go to San Diego the day after tomorrow." I said. "I mean the day after today, I guess. Tomorrow."

I called Kendall Lea from Isaiah's and told her I'd be right home.

"Is Isaiah okay?" she asked.

"No."

"Oh god, what?"

"I'll tell you when I get there."

Taxbreak said he'd drive Raphael home, so I went straight to the apartment. Kendall Lea threw open the door as I was walking up the steps. She was in a bathrobe. She hugged me at the top of the stairs and we went inside, her arm around my waist. "So . . . how, what?"

"Real bad news. Isaiah went back on the stuff. We found him in some sleaze bar and took him home. He's dead."

"Oh God. Oh God. Oh God." Kendall Lea sank into a chair. I fixed two Canadian whiskeys, and she took hers distractedly. "How did it happen?"

I explained the whole thing, just as I had to the police, leaving out the bit about the trance, but telling her about the weird voice Isaiah was yelling in. Kendall Lea just stared vacantly in front of her.

"Did he put himself into a trance?" she asked.

"I don't know. Maybe. Hard for me to tell."

"He did, didn't he?"

"I thought so at the time, but he could have just been in a—I don't know what you call it when some guy has O.D.'d."

Kendall Lea took a deep breath, let it out, and stared ahead.

"This is just awful. Awful." She stared blindly across the room and her eyes glistened damply. We sat there for about five minutes, saying nothing. I pulled out the gold pocket watch she had given me. It was a few minutes after six.

"Are his parents alive?" she asked.

"I don't know."

"You better find out," she said. Yeah, I thought, they'd have to ship the body home most likely, after it had been autopsied. The front office wouldn't open until nine. It would be a little after eight o'clock on the East Coast. I went over to the phone and got the number for N. C. State from information. Someone answered and I asked for Ralph Freeland, the basketball coach there. College coaches usually keep better hours than professional ones, and Freeland answered. I had met him a few years ago at some banquet and he remembered me right away.

"How's our boy Isaiah doin'?" he drawled.

"That's what I'm calling about, coach. Bad news. He'd been on coke and—"

"What?"

"Cocaine. And we'd got him off it but last night he went out and got a snootful. We found him and took him to his place and he had a kind of fit and fell in the bathroom. Hit his head. He's dead."

"Holy Mother of God."

"Real bad, real bad."

"Lord, you never know. He was such a fine boy. Such an athlete. God, sometimes I feel like Satan, sending boys up to you guys. Country boys. They don't know what to do with all that money, all that . . . well, damn it. Damn it all."

"Yeah, I'm sorry. He was a great player. Look, coach, I'm going to have to let his family know. Do you know how to reach them? I'm sorry to bother you with . . . "

"No, that's okay. Let's see, if I remember right his father's dead. Yeah, died three years ago in an auto accident. Damn fool was drunk. His stepmother's still alive, lives up in Halifax County, Virginia, in a big house Isaiah had built for her and his daddy. Wait a minute. I think I can get the number. Hold on."

I waited.

"Here you go. Mrs. William Jones. Name's Delia." He read off a number, and I wrote it down. "You want me to call her? I met her a couple of times. Back when Isaiah was playing here."

"No, that's okay, Coach," I said. "I better do it myself. I'm much obliged. Oh, hey, what about the mother? Is she alive?"

"No, she died when Isaiah was a kid, just an infant, about one and a half. Some kind of household accident. His stepmother is all the family he has. I mean had."

"Okay. Sorry to call you with such bad news."

"The Lord's will," said Coach Freeland and hung up.

I called Tub Bligh at his home and filled him in. He said he would take over all of the details, that I should concentrate on basketball if it was humanly possible, and that he hoped that I was okay.

"Yeah, I guess so." I said.

"Have you called his family yet?" asked Tub Bligh.

"No not yet. I found out from the coach at N. C. State

he's only got a stepmother left. No other family."

"A lonely man."

"Yessir. Very much so it seems."

"I'll take care of giving her the bad news." Tub said.

"Thank you, sir. Her name is Mrs. William Jones. Delia Jones." I gave him the number.

"All right, son. I'll take care of it. God, this is tragic. A tragic season. Jim Munson, Isaiah. Well, get some rest if you can. I'll talk to you later."

"Thanks. I'll be at the arena at ten."

Kendall Lea was still sitting in the chair, her drink untouched. "Was Isaiah's father named William?" she asked.

"Yeah. It seems so." It seemed unimportant. I was numb.

There was a knock on the door.

"And his mother?"

I went across the room to the door. "Dead. Died when he was a little kid." I opened the door. It was Taxbreak and his wife, Lucia, who was carrying a large paper bag.

"I will make your breakfast. Without sleep it is even more important." She went into the kitchen and I followed Taxbreak into the living room. Everything seemed to be taking place in slow motion. It was like watching someone else's movie.

"I talked to the police. The medical examiner said if he hadn't hit his head, he probably would have died anyway. He had enough alcohol and coke in him to stop most men's hearts." Taxbreak sat down across from Kendall Lea. "Don't start thinking that . . . "

"I know what happened," said Kendall Lea in a quiet, almost mechanical voice. Her eyes were full of tears.

"I do too," said Taxbreak. "He backslid, went and over-dosed himself, had a fit, and hit his head. It's one of those things, awful, but they happen. Usually just when you least expect it."

"No, there's more to it than that," said Kendall Lea, still staring off into the distance. "I'm sure I know what happened." Lucia stood in the doorway to the kitchen. "When he was shouting in that strange voice and acting as if he was being hit, he was acting out something, something awful, and I'm sure I know what it was. His mother died when he was a little baby."

"That's right," I said. "The coach at N. C. State said he was about one and a half. A household accident."

"His father's name," Kendall Lea went on, "was William."

"He died a couple of years ago. Drunk."

"Yes," said Kendall Lea. "He was probably always an alcoholic. And when Isaiah was a little boy, his father—Billy—beat his mother to death before his eyes. She was probably pregnant. It was something he obviously had blocked out of his conscious mind, something too terrible to know. It was put in the records as an accident, a fall in the bathroom, or something like that. Isaiah was acting that out."

"Kendall, that seems pretty far-fetched to me," I said. "C'mon . . . "

"It fits. It fits too well."

"So what all of a sudden triggered the memory of it. The coke?"

"No," Kendall Lea said. Her eyes watered again. "Hypnosis."

"Come *on*, Kendall." I shouted. I had a headache, and my eyes itched. I was suddenly struck with an odd sense of fear.

"He never said where he was going when he was in a trance. He didn't know where he was going. He was just pushing things back. I taught him to put himself into a trance. And he just kept probing, until he found it, his mother's murder, and it was too much for him. He went crazy, and then—you said he seemed to go off in a trance just before he began shouting in a woman's voice, didn't you? That's probably when he saw it again. He acted it out. He was a man who used his body to express himself."

"Wait a minute," I said. I felt like I was fighting gravity, the way you can't make yourself run when you're dreaming. "I thought you said the unconcious mind would always protect a guy from anything bad like that."

"Something went wrong. Something went wrong. Maybe I taught him wrong. I don't know." Tears streamed down her face.

Lucia spoke quietly from the door. "You cannot blame yourself for this, Kendall, *chicita*. He was possessed by a spirit, my little one."

"Lucia," said Taxbreak. "Don't start that stuff. It won't help."

"Listen," said Lucia to her husband. "You are a man of science. You can fix bodies, like mechanics fix engines. Very good. You do not believe certain things, but my people have been here a long time and we know of other worlds. If what Kendall has said is true, then it is obvious to me that the mother's spirit was trapped when she was killed and awaited the chance to enter her son's body and reenact her own death—to be free."

"Lucia, that's crap," said Taxbreak.

"You may believe your science. I will believe what I know to be true."

Lucia crossed the room and knelt in front of Kendall Lea, taking her hands. "These things are beyond anyone's control, *chicita*."

Kendall Lea put her hands up, as if to push something away. She shook her head. "No, no, no. It's too strong, too dangerous! I . . . oh, damn."

"Come," said the little woman. "Wash your face. We can eat now."

Nobody seemed to be hungry, picking at Lucia's *heuvos rancheros.* I drank a beer. The rest of the day was a fog, explaining to the press that Isaiah's death was an accidental fall in the bathroom, letting the guys know it was a fall occasioned by an overdose, trying to run a practice, trying to concentrate when my mind was fixed on the tears that had run down Kendall Lea's face, and a sense of foreboding. The bottom was falling out. It was like clinging to a huge spinning top, knowing that you were about to lose your grip and be flung off into somewhere. I slept like a sunken log that night.

The next morning, after a silent breakfast, I stood up and said: "Well, let's pack. The goddamned season waits for no man."

"I'm not coming," said Kendall Lea, and my stomach turned over. I thought I was going to throw up.

"What do you mean?"

She looked up and took my hand. "I've got to think. I'll just stay here. You'll be back in two days." She squeezed my hand and I felt cold.

16 THE GUYS sat on the airplane in their usual configurations, cramped and out of kilter with the rest of the world, knees and ankles jutting out into the aisle, mostly lying back with head phones, knowing that they were the focus of nervous attention, other guys with bankers' suits wondering if they could get up the nerve to stand up and walk down the aisle and ask Raphael Flint—I mean, Buffie, honey, I talked to Raphael Flint!—for his autograph. The guys looked cool, a natural act, well, maybe not natural but assumed when as boys they reached six foot before their time and gangled over the rest of the world, giants of a specialized sort, freaks. We were the freak show. I remembered once when the Barnum and Bailey Circus came to Denver and my father and mother took me to it and I forgot all the acrobatics and the pink uniforms and the lavender tutus and the young/old hags astride lealthery elephants because I was so taken with the freaks. Dwarfs. Giants. Fat ladies. So here I was, on an airplane, shot like a rocket into the sky with jillions of gallons on fuel, hurtling with my own group of freaks and performers into a trajectory that would wind up like a NASA program in San Diego, and my freaks, my circus, would get out of the plane and shuffle in their titanic manner off to some nameless hotel and tomorrow play the game of basketball so the the networks and the freaks might get wealthy. . . . I had a lot of cynical thoughts that night, of course, all brought on by the simple fact that I had seen Kendall Lea whom I loved beyond imagination in a mood that I could not think about. And Isaiah was dead.

Dead. I mean, the guy was gone forever, smoke, ashes, vapor. Isaiah, whom I didn't like that much but needed in the line-up, was gone. Gone. It takes awhile to know a guy is dead. Big word, that: *forever.*

Two nights ago I had seen Isaiah jitter-step, feint, fake a step, turn on the afterburner, and sail past a big man and gently lose the ball to the forces of aerodynamics, already understood and in place before he moved, and the ball simply sighed through the threads. Now he was no more. Nothing left. And Kendall Lea was crying in my apartment and I was in a stupid motherfucking cigar-shaped airplane hurtling through the foul air of Southern California herding a bunch of egomaniacal freaks who played some abstract form of the game of life and I was lost, I mean to tell you, lost. Terrified.

We lost in San Diego and I called Tub and said, "We lost. Don't tell me. We're still going to the play-offs." And I hung up as he said, "Son . . . ?"

We also lost to Golden State and then we went home. Before both games I called home, that is my apartment (I had to look up the number because I practically never called my apartment) and there was no one there and I was certain that Kendall Lea had gone, vanished . . . do you know what I mean? She wasn't there. I got mad. I got two technical fouls in the fourth quarter when we were playing Golden State and was thrown out of the arena. "Bullshit" is what I said when the fat little ref threw me out and they called a third technical foul on me. Raphael started to reach for me and I told him I didn't want to hear any god-damned homilies from a Detroit felon. He glared at me and I left.

I was messed up. Thank God the plane got us back to Albuquerque without an explosion of some sort. I stepped off the plane onto the tarmac of the airport and found my way along with the others to the entrance from the runway, and walked down the long, tiled hallway, boots clicking. The kachinas depicted on the walls stared vacantly, icons of an old and guilt-tripping, remorse-producing religion. In the lobby, I said, "Hey, Raphael, I'll see you tomorrow."

He stopped, his canvas bag over his shoulder, and said, "I'm sure looking forward to it."

The Checker was hot inside. It was spring and it was getting warm and the southwestern sun had left its testimony to solar heating. I opened the windows and drove out of the long-term parking area and eased down Gibson Street to the freeway, happy to know at least that what I was dreading I would soon find or not find. It was ten o'clock. Post meridian, I think is what they call it. I found myself in an unconscious fury and tried to let my hands grasp the wheel more gently. They wouldn't. I worried over a dumb play I had sent in against Golden State, and I panicked about Kendall Lea. She'd left. No forwarding address. A goddamn outrage, after all I'd done, all I'd given, and her damn ferns all over the place and the water spilled all over the floor watering the goddamned ferns and . . . oh, Christ, I hope she's there.

She was. She was sitting on the sofa, dressed in a reddish-pink shirt—blouse, what do I know?—and she was surrounded with a bunch of canvas bags.

"What the hell is all this?" I asked.

"My stuff."

"I know it's your stuff. Don't be stupid. I know it's your stuff and I know you've got some damn bee in your bonnet and I don't like it."

"I'm leaving," she said and looked at me with eyes that were as deep and humid as the ocean.

"No you're not!" I said.

"I have to. I have to go. No, don't come over here, don't. I have to go. I just wanted to tell you face to face."

"Thanks a hell of a lot. I don't want to hear it."

"Look," she said. "Understand. I killed a man. I came here with an idea—an ideal—and I ruined it. Do you hear? I ruined it."

"Don't give me that crap, goddamn it. You . . . "

"Look, there's a big mess here and I made it and I have to go away and . . . "

"Bullshit!"

"*Stop* that! Understand? I can't be here anymore. I played the wrong game. I took your enthusiasm as straightforward and . . . I *killed* a man. If you hadn't wanted to get into the goddam play-offs so badly . . . I . . . look, believe me, I don't belong here right now, I have to think. I need . . . I can't stand this."

She was pushing things away with her hands again.

I said: "Kendall, stay here for now. For tonight. Let's talk about it later, I mean, we . . . you and me . . . we're sort of . . . "

She began to talk in that mechanical voice I hated. "I," she said, "have created a monster here in our lives and I'm going to have to deal with that all my life and I am going to go and think for a while and not be pushed around— jerked around—by all your shitty ambitions. Do you hear me?"

"But, Kendall," I said, "It was you, in Portland, who said . . ."

"That was a long time ago." She stood up and picked up her bags. She struggled out of the house and down the steps to the lilac Cadillac and tossed the bags into the back seat and drove off. It was dark and the lights of Albuquerque glittered like diamonds in a soft black velvet saucer and I retched once in my throat, shouted, "Goddamn you," and retched again. I hadn't eaten anything since breakfast so nothing soiled the rug when I vomited air and pain. I sat down on the rug and coughed and then I cried, the awful, humiliating, salty tears erupting from my eyes as I swore and stared into an abyss filled with horrors and emptiness, the loss of all losses, an infuriating, suffocating, irrevocable descent into quicksand, the way I knew even as a little boy that I would one day die: betrayed.

17 THE NEXT MORNING when I got to the arena, Raphael was sitting in my office, looking at some notes on a clipboard.

"She's gone, Raphael."

He looked up. "Gone?"

"Vamoosed."

"Where?"

I moved around the desk and sat down. "I don't know."

"We got eight more games," said the big man. "San Antonio has the bad part of the schedule—they're playing all tough teams. We've only got one game with a play-off contender."

"So we have a chance," I said.

"Not if you're going to act crazy, we don't." Raphael stood up and leaned on the desk, staring down at me. "You coaches are always telling us to concentrate . . . "

"You're a coach, too," I interrupted.

"And I am telling you to concentrate, boy. You hear? You put everything out of your mind except how to keep this team alive. We're entitled to that. We've worked our butts off for you this season and you"—he jabbed me with a long black finger—"owe us. *You . . . owe . . . us.*" He turned and went out of the room.

We won four and lost four. San Antonio, with a surge of playing over their heads, won four and lost four. It wasn't enough. They finished one game behind us. We had backed into the play-offs. The guys, watching San Antonio lose their last game of the season, shouted and joshed each other, and threw stuff around the locker room and Tub Bligh hugged his freaks and laughed and told me that he would live up to his promise, and I joined in the merriment with a big wide phoney grin and I felt empty. In two days, we would go off to Seattle for the first round of the play-offs, a three-game series. Dumfrey Schwartz was waddling around the locker room with an exultant look on his face as if his inspired prose had made the difference to the Demon's play-off hopes. I thought of Kendall Lea and wondered, if everything hadn't gone sour, whether she would have broken her rule and joined the guys in the locker room for the celebration. I felt myself getting mad and tried to think of something else.

We went to Seattle for the first round of the play-offs. I concentrated like I'd never done before, catching myself just before I'd start to think of Kendall Lea and get pissed off, saying little homilies to myself about thinking only about basketball. You know how it feels when you've got a little nick on the inside of your cheek, or maybe a filling that's gotten broken, and you try to keep your tongue away from it and you concentrate on holding your tongue down there against your lower teeth so it won't start worrying the nick or the filling and, as soon as you take your mind off it, your tongue is right back at it. And while I tried in Seattle to keep my mind on working out tactics to keep our guys from falling behind, my mind kept lurching back to Kendall and I would find myself swearing. Out loud even. In the third quarter, when we were behind by ten and things were getting worse, I found myself looking around in the stands hoping to spot Kendall sitting up there with a book or something like in Seattle a hundred years ago wearing her pink blouse, staring intently at the flow of freaks on the hardwood, and said shit, I guess for the eleventh time, and the referee saddled me with a technical foul, so I concentrated on basketball and we lost anyway.

Two nights later, back in Albuquerque, the game was a street brawl from the beginning to the end—all to the accompaniment of the fans' well-rehearsed mayhem, and the whole damn time there was this bruise lurking somewhere in me, maybe more like a hole, and the worse the brawl on the floor got, the madder I got. Just before the final buzzer, Mo Flynn fouled out on a dumb play and Seattle tied it up so we went into overtime and lost by three points. The season was over.

Probably you don't know how that feels.

We'd been last in our division—last in the league, in fact—in December and after all those nights and all those miles and all those moments and bruises and swollen joints and all that insane screaming of Deeeeemon-State, it was over. For months there's everything. Then there's nothing. Other guys would go on through the play-offs into the championship series and some team—probably the goddam Lakers—would win it and be heroes and by then we would all be sitting somewhere on our asses wondering what the hell to do with ourselves.

Sure, I'd be head coach next season, with a slightly fatter contract. A step up the Big Ladder, with a few local commentators saying that the Demons had pulled off a minor miracle but what the hell did they know? Our starting point guard was dead, Raphael would probably retire, we had a play-off team that had to start rebuilding right away. Have to hire another fucking hypnotist. The tongue probed the stupid flaw in my mouth and I told the guys they'd been wonderful and all that and went home to the apartment and—I swear it was a mistake—knocked over one of Kendall's goddamned ferns. I let it lie, had three glasses of Scotch and went to bed.

The next day I called a real estate agent and put the apartment up for sale. I didn't like it there anymore. I took all the damn ferns over to Raphael's house and asked him if Dora would water them. I was going away for a few days. I told Raphael that Tub Bligh was going to name me head coach.

"That's good, man," said Raphael. He was sitting in a vastly oversized chair that looked the right size with him in it. His house was very clean, very sparsely furnished. The collection of ferns looked like a small jungle in his living room.

"A real big shot now," Raphael said.

"Nah."

"Management."

"I guess so," I said. "Lots of decisions to make."

Raphael sat impassively in the huge chair.

"Are you going to join me?" I asked.

"As assistant coach?"

"As playing assistant coach."

Raphael looked at me, and then looked away.

"Dora?" he shouted. "This white man has offered me my job again."

From the kitchen, Dora answered. "Take it."

"Do I get a raise?" asked Raphael.

"A *raise?* You greedy bastard. I'm offering you status. You're already filthy rich."

"Well," said Raphael, putting his long fingers together in an arch, "I like telling these assholes what to do. Yeah, I'm in."

"Do you always ask Dora about this kind of thing?"

"Wouldn't you?" the big man asked, then said: "Oh, hey, I'm sorry."

I felt anger in my throat. "Don't worry about that, Raphael." I got up and shook his hand. "I'll be back in a few days. Sorry to dump all these ferns on you."

"Ferns don't bother me none," said the big man. He paused as if he was going to say something else, and then stood up. "See you in a few days, boss man."

Three days later I was sitting next to a stream that raced—cold and clear—down a gorge lined with gigantic dark spruces and pines. Pure Rocky Mountain spring water. I fished my last can of Coors out of the icy water and popped it open. The stream was a mountain tributary to the White River, which has its beginnings in the mountains of the White River National Forest, north of Glenwood Springs, Colorado. It was cool, almost cold, and a thousand or so feet above me was snow. Beside me, on the blanket of needles under the trees, was my pack and an old Winchester .30-30 my father had given me when I turned fourteen. It had been his father's. The sun, streaming through the boughs overhead, separated into what seemed individual rays by the drooping branches, glinted off the blue-back barrel of the rifle. I picked it up and nudged the safety off and aimed at a long, drooping pine cone about forty yards away. *Blam!* The sound reverberated in the woods long after I saw I'd missed. I shrugged and put the rifle down. I'd been in the woods two days now. I'd hiked up to the snow line and then back down to this place beside the stream and had made camp here. By now it felt like home. There was a squirrel who had spent most of his time reminding me noisily that it was his home first. He was overhead now, chittering bitchily, pissed off by the sound of the rifle.

"Shut up, stupid," I said.

Chitter.

"Okay. A deal," I said. "You don't bug me, I won't bug you."

Chitter.

"Okay. No deal."

The smell of the spruces and the rotting needles on the ground was pungent, clean. The sun on my neck was warm. Below me, in the gorge, the stream rushed by, swirling and dancing in the rocks, eroding them imperceptibly. I felt empty, reamed out. Lonely. I yearned to show this place to Kendall Lea, to watch her poke around the side of the stream like a stork, and I felt a kind of pinching behind my eyes. Goddamn it. Goddamn it. I was mad again. My eyes—my vision—seemed to be shutting down from outside in, like someone was setting the aperture of a lens to accommodate a bright light. The pine cone I had missed seemed to stand out in sharp relief. I picked up the Winchester, worked the lever, and aimed. *Blam!* Missed again. Chitter, chitter from overhead. "Shit," I said and stood up.

I took a length of rope from my pack, tied one end to a small rock and threw it over a branch about ten feet off the ground. Basket high. Then I fed the other end through one strap on the pack and made a knot so that the pack swung about seven feet off the ground. The squirrel was silent. I looked up but couldn't see him in the tree. Uphill were simply more big spruces, more soft, needle-covered slopes. Downhill the same. I went up, making my way through the tall evergreens and the silence. There was a loud squawk and, in the clearing where the stream coursed down the mountain, I saw a gray and black bird sail by. A Clark's nutcracker. I had read somewhere that those birds buried thousands of nuts all over the place and somehow remembered every place and would retrieve them later—all of them.

Kendall Lea, I thought, had never seen one of those. The hell with her, I thought, think of something else. Sure, but what? I stopped and looked up. A slight breeze was moving the drooping spruce boughs, sighing ever so softly, a distant sound. Otherwise, silence. I felt stupid. Usually when I came out to the woods and wandered for a day or two, I was able to put all thoughts, all concerns, out of mind, to become as nearly as possible another mindless part of the woods, as patient as the trees, waiting for nothing. But now I still chittered like the squirrel at the angry bruise somewhere inside me, the bruise that surrounded a great emptiness.

A hundred yards farther up the slope there was a small clearing surrounded by towering spruces. I set the Winchester down and lay back in the pine needles, my hands behind my head. The sun was slightly to the west, warming me in the cool air. On the ground, there was no movement of air but overhead the breeze ruffled the branches, sighing. After a few minutes I went to sleep.

I woke up and recognized the place. There was a particularly tall spruce between me and the sun and the sunlight streamed through its needles. Its boughs hung down, silent and strong. From far off, above me, a flicker called, a call of certitude and hope. The flicker was at home in the forest. The unimaginably tall tree loomed up, filtering the sunlight, valiant, patient, knowing the needs of woodpeckers and soil and air. Behind the tree the sky was cerulean, pure, and the only sound I could hear was the sound of my own breathing, cool air coursing into my bloodstream. I could feel the blood moving through my veins.

Somewhere far off I heard another sound, another voice, a soft voice. It was saying something I couldn't quite make out. I listened. "This is your place," it said. "A place where you will always know peace." I listened to my breathing and I heard the flicker call again. "And now in your own time," the voice said and drifted off and the cerulean sky began to turn into a hotel room, I was rising through gravity and before me Kendall Lea sat, her face quiet, her dark sapphire eyes in repose, little lines of smiles and age creating a geologic setting for the glistening gems, and I realized I was back in Portland. It was December and the whole thing was a dream, the whole season, the . . . the everything, Jim Munson, Isaiah, Kendall living with me, betraying me by leaving, all a hypnotic trance, and I burst into tears and thought this is pretty stupid—an assistant coach in the NBA crying in front of a lady he hardly knows. But wait, I thought. I'm head coach. I know that lady. I know her like I know the veins on the back of my hand. I've made love to her and soared with her and . . . Goddamn it, Goddamn it! I opened my eyes and the unimaginably tall spruce tree was there. It hadn't moved. I was lying on the pine-needle blanket in the clearing, looking up at the tree. I reached and felt the Winchester next to me. I stood up. A few feet away was a gray rock. I kicked it and it hopped into the middle of the clearing.

"Take that, you motherfucking bishop."

I picked up the rifle and set out down the slope.

The next morning I woke up in a motel in Denver, the first one I had found the night before. I never did know the name of the place. I had a late breakfast amidst the universal decor of motel coffee shops, read in the Denver *Post* that the world was going to hell as usual, and didn't care a damned bit. Back in my room I called information in New York City, got the number for the Morgan Guaranty bank and dialed it. A voice answered.

"Mr. Lea, please. He's a vice president in the main office."

"Yes, I know." The phone buzzed genteelly.

I had met Kendall Lea's father once, about two months before when we were in New York to play the Knicks. He was a jovial man, self-assured, with a haw-haw laugh you associate with guys who belong to men's clubs. We'd met at the Yale Club and he'd bought us drinks before the game. I was surprised. He seemed genuinely interested in the Demons and asked a lot of good questions that you wouldn't expect. Professional athletes are not exactly what you think of as upper crust, even thought they often make more money than the old-monied types like Kendall's father, but he had seemed amused that Kendall was working with us.

"Lea here."

"Mr. Lea?" I identified myself.

"Oh, yes. How are you? I see that you made the play-offs."

"Barely."

"You're calling about Kendall, I imagine."

"Yes, sir. I need to talk to her. She and I . . . well, we've been through a lot together and some of it was pretty bad. She's blaming herself for something that nobody can take responsibility for. I need to talk to her."

"I think that would be a good idea. Her mother and I have spoken with her once or twice on the phone since she . . . uh . . . returned and she does not sound happy at all. She's in Chincoteague."

"Chincoteague?"

"On the east coast of Virginia. She's at the Refuge Motor Inn, but there are no phones in the rooms. You can leave a message for her with the office."

"Thank you, sir. Thanks very much."

"Stay in touch," said the banker and hung up.

An hour later I was on a plane to Washington, D.C. At Dulles Airport I rented a car, bought a Rand-McNally road atlas and set out for Chincoteague, about four, maybe five hours away. The time zones were against me: it was six-thirty on the East coast. I got to Chincoteague at about eleven o'clock, the last mile or so being a long causeway through marshland and inlet, black water that reflected the stars. In the town a traffic light blinked and some dreary-looking buildings lined the street. Most of the buildings were dark. I drove around and finally found Kendall's motel on the edge of town just before a bridge that led over some more water to the Chincoteague National Wildlife Refuge. The office at the motel was shut, dark. In the parking lot I saw Kendall's lilac Cadillac. I stopped the rental car, got out, and went over to the convertible. Its fender was smooth and cold. Overhead were stars and the breeze was swishing through some dark pines around the perimeter of the parking lot. "Okay," I said out loud. "Okay."

I went back into town and found a motel room for the night.

18 I WOKE UP with the first light, drank a cup of machine coffee, and drove out of town to the Refuge Motor Inn. It was a day of nearly crystalline clarity, with a breeze blowing snappily inland from the ocean. I panicked for a moment when I didn't see the lilac Cadillac in the motel lot. The office was closed, wouldn't open till eight, a sign said, so I figured she couldn't have checked out. In fact, she could have. She could have checked out the night before and left before dawn. But I didn't want to think about that so I figured she hadn't checked out.

The road past the motel leads to a bridge that takes you into the Chincoteague National Wildlife Refuge. I nosed along, passing between stands of pines that were swaying slightly in the breeze. After a few hundred yards, there was a big parking lot on the left and among the handful of cars in it was the Cadillac. I pulled up beside it and looked inside. There was a pair of knitted purple gloves on the dashboard. A well-marked path led off through a grove of pines. Tiny little birds were flitting around in the trees—yellow ones and black and white ones. Warblers, I guessed. You don't see too many warblers in the Southwest.

The path led out to a paved road beyond which marshland stretched away toward the ocean, acres and acres of grass and water. I walked along the road, heading north, past the swaying marsh grass. Out in the water were ducks,

hundreds of them bobbing and swaying in the slight chop.
The wind was a constant swishing sound. A few hundred
yards down the road there was a long narrow piece of dry
land that looked as if it bisected the marsh, and I turned
and walked along it. There were seagulls and terns plying
the marsh, swooping down and up, crying out, a melancholy sound. The seashore tends to make me feel a bit melancholy—especially the sound of seagulls. The trail turned
to the right as it passed through a grove of pines, and about
a hundred yards away, standing in the dry brown grass at
the end of the promontory, in a suede jacket and blue jeans
with her yellow hair blowing in the wind, was Kendall Lea.
Unmistakably Kendall Lea. She was looking out over the
marsh with a pair of binoculars, still as a post except for
her hair. I felt dizzy, I couldn't breathe. I reached out and
held a pine branch until my breathing got back to normal.
For a few minutes—I don't know how long—I stood and
watched Kendall Lea. I tried to see what she was looking at
out on the water. I could make out some little white specks,
way out across the water. The sun, just up over the horizon, lit up Kendall Lea like a halo.

I set off down the promontory, walking carefully, quietly, as if I were stalking a deer. About ten yards from her
I stopped.

"Aha," I said.

She took the binoculars from her eyes and turned.

"I found you," I said.

A smile flickered and went. She looked down, then up.
Her face was . . . quiet.

"Hi," she said. "Hey. . . ." Now, in a situation like this the
words "hi" and "hey" may not seem the most eloquent things
you ever heard, but they seemed just fine to me.

"Hi," I replied.

"You made the play-offs." she said.

"Yeah."

"And you're head coach." Small talk, like her father, I thought. I felt myself beginning to bristle.

"Yeah, I will be." I said. "But that's not the point."

"I've missed you so much."

"Same here, babe."

"I was so scared."

"Yep. Me, too."

"I wasn't thinking very well. I was really scared. So I got angry."

"Scared that Isaiah was your fault," I said.

"Yes, of course." The wind blew her golden hair back and forth over her eyes. "But I've decided he wasn't my fault. He was everybody's fault. Or nobody's."

"I don't think I understand," I said.

"He was antisocial. Like a criminal. No one knows why criminals are like that, but they are. They look at the world as being unfair, a place where they have to look out only for number one. Even when they cooperate with the world, it's for their own gain and no one else's. Isaiah was like that. No friends. He couldn't have friends. Inside, in the core, he was just empty."

Way out beyond the copper-colored grass, the little white specks took flight and vanished.

"Probably his mother's death made him that way," she said. "I don't know. I don't know why he would have wanted to push back and find that out."

" "Do you believe any of that spirit stuff that Lucia was talking about?"

"Some people do. If it is true, then it was one of the few generous acts—truly generous acts—in Isaiah's life."

"Huh?"

"People who believe in that spiritual stuff believe that a trance state is an ideal place for a spirit to enter someone, to possess someone. If Lucia was right about all that, then Isaiah somehow was offering himself up to his mother so she could be free. We'll never know."

A black and white tern flew past, beating its way into the breeze. Kendall Lea smiled sadly at me across the ten yards of brown grass. Her hair blew across her face.

"I love you," I said. Her eyes glistened.

"I said some awful things to you," she said.

"And you ran out. I felt betrayed."

"What did you do?" she asked.

"I did what any red-blooded former Boy Scout would do. I felt sorry for myself." She laughed. "So I went to the woods for a couple of days, had myself a little vision like the Indians do—you know, self-deprivation. An ordeal. I ran out of beer, for Chrissakes."

"What was your vision?"

"*You,* dummy. You. So here I am. And there you are. Too far away. Let's get married."

"I think that would be lovely," she said. I had gotten over fainting when she said stuff like that. She had begun as a piece of pure magic. Now she was merely real. I walked over to her and she put her arms around my neck.

"I love you, big man. I want to be your wife."

Out in the marsh something set off the ducks. They took off in chaos, quacking, wheeled as one and flew across the promontory.

"See," I said. "I told you way back in Seattle that we were going to have grandchildren."

"You always have been one to plan ahead," she said and put her arm in mine. "You want to look at some snow geese?"

"I want to look at your motel room."

We walked down the promontory and the breeze blew Kendall Lea's hair and the gulls cried out and it didn't seem melancholy at all.

We took five days to drive the two thousand-odd miles back to Albuquerque in the lilac Cadillac. Must of used a supertanker worth of gasoline. We took a northerly route so we wouldn't have to drive through the endless wastes of Texas. The last night on the road, in a motel in Taos, I explained that I had taken her ferns to Raphael's place, so she shouldn't be shocked by their absence. I also told her I'd put the apartment on the block, that I'd done it in my funk.

"I'm sorry," she said.

"*I'm* not. Anyway we agreed that we weren't going to be sorry about all that crap. We're going to need a bigger place anyway, when you . . . I mean you could easily get pregnant, you know. It happens."

"Wrong tense," she said and lay back in the bed with her hands behind her head. I sat up and looked at her. "It seems," she said with a beatific smile, "that I am possessed by a tiny little demon."

"Holy shit!" I believe that is what I said as she turned out the light and took me into her warm strong arms.

"He'll play shooting guard," she said.

We got into Albuquerque about noon the next day and I put our stuff in the apartment and told her I'd go down to the arena and check in and be back in a couple of hours.

"I'll start the house search," she said. "How many rooms?"

"Let's see." I said. "Why don't you count up the number of kids you want and multiply by four? I don't want to have to move all the time." I kissed her and headed for the door. "Oh yeah. Find one with tile floors."

"Why tile floors?"

"The ferns, beautiful, the ferns. They have to be watered."

She slugged me on the arm. "Okay, one tile-floored nest coming up. What about a dog?"

Forty-five minutes later, I was sitting in my office, staring at a contract Tub Bligh had sent over for the job of head coach, when Raphael Flint walked past the door and then reappeared.

"Hey," he said. "You're back." He leaned against the wall.

"Yeah, I'm back."

"Good trip?"

"Raphael, we're going to get married."

"What you talkin about, man? I'm already married."

"Me and Kendall Lea, you damned oaf. Tomorrow. At Taxbreak's ranch. I've volunteered you as best man."

Then a miracle happened. Well, as a matter of fact, I don't believe in miracles anymore. Wonderful things can happen, that's for damn sure, but they take a lot of hard work and more luck. But what happened at one o'clock that day in my office in the arena where the Albuquerque Demons play some forty games of basketball each year, was probably the sort of event that, if you stretch the rules a little, you could classify as a minor miracle.

For one nanosecond, Raphael Flint *smiled*.